Lynn Lauber's
WHITE GIRLS

"Portrays small-town Ohio life with wit and a sharp social consciousness. Lynn Lauber has an acute eye for absurdities and a wonderful sense of humor that takes none of the edges off her barbed observations... A fine debut from a talented new writer."
—*Newsday*

"An insightful and often painful portrayal of female adolescence told in a wry and sensitive voice."
—Mary McGarry Morris

"Growing up restless in a small town is a common theme of American literature. [Lauber] takes that same theme, injects it with a fresh note and presents us with a memorable story."
—*San Francisco Examiner-Chronicle*

"Lauber's perfect recall of a 'bad' girl's surly moods... [is] worth the price of admission....One of the sharpest debut collections we've read in a while."
—*Glamour*

"A fine account of what it's like to grow up [as] an adolescent whose emerging sexuality can find neither the space nor the guidelines it needs."
—*USA Today*

White Girls

WHITE GIRLS

◆

Lynn Lauber

VINTAGE CONTEMPORARIES
Vintage Books
A Division of Random House, Inc.
New York

FIRST VINTAGE CONTEMPORARIES EDITION, SEPTEMBER 1991

Acknowledgment is made to the following publications in which these stories
first appeared: "Sugar Street" in *Fiction Network*; "In The Country" in
The Tie That Binds (Papier-Mache' Press); "Wearing Green" in *Other Voices*;
"Specialists" in *Pax*; and "White Girls" in *Stories*.

Lyrics from the following songs have been used: "Yes! We Have No Bananas"
© 1923 Skidmore Music Company Inc. New York. Copyright renewed.
"Run to Him" (G. Goffin/J. Keller) © 1961 Screen Gems-EMI Music Inc.
and Colgems-EMI Music Inc. "In a Shanty in Old Shanty Town,"
by Little Jack Little, John Siras and Joe Young. © 1923 Warner Bros. Inc.
(Renewed). All Rights Reserved. Used by Permission.

Library of Congress Cataloging-in-Publication Data
Lauber, Lynn.
White girls: stories / Lynn Lauber. — 1st Vintage contemporaries ed.
p.   cm. — (Vintage contemporaries)
ISBN 0-679-73411-2 (pbk.)
I. Title.
[PS3562.A784W4   1991]
813'.54—dc20   91-50012
CIP

For
my grandmother,
my mother
& my daughter

Contents

Part II   Sugar Street

White Girls

South Rosewood Avenue

ALTHOUGH none of us knew who he was then and most of us never learned later, we attended a grade school in Union, Ohio, named after Marcus Aurelius. His name became as common to us as Homer, a village to our east that specialized in bait, and Morocco, a town in Indiana where one of my aunts had moved when it became clear she'd never marry. We already had our view of Caesar, a pizza parlor on Calumet that specialized in lasagna, and the Forum, where we bought my orthopedic shoes. It was not our fault that at Marcus Aurelius, world history only went back to the Civil War, that our imaginations stopped at the Atlantic beaches, near Maine. Still, even deep in Ohio someone remembered the Parthenon, recalled a line from the *Iliad*, possessed a gene from the Roman Empire. Even deep in Ohio, with no water to look at, people bending in cornfields, standing on corners were known to smell something salty and ancient, and be inspired.

In Marcus Aurelius, the ceilings were low, and the floors made so slick by the black janitor, Mr. Jefferson, that visitors from the PTA often slipped and fell on their tailbones when they came inside. Mr. Jefferson was the only adult who anyone could order around. He had three children at Marcus Aurelius, all named something exotic. Parthena was the girl my age, long-legged with great beige teeth, and like all blacks in our school, she walked the margins of the halls buffed by her father, expecting nothing from anyone.

The Jeffersons lived on another branch of the street we'd just moved to, Rosewood Avenue, but a branch more chaotic, unmowed—interesting, I thought. There, babies wearing diapers played on front yards in full view of traffic; women leaned their torsos out of open windows to call to men who were leaving before they were supposed to; children sat, white plates on black knees, and ate fried suppers.

We drove through this branch of Rosewood in order to reach Market Street, which took us to most of the destinations of our lives—to Unity Methodist Church on Sundays and for mother/daughter banquets; to Gregg's, the department store downtown, where we bought the stiff floral material for the school dresses my mother sewed out of duty each year; to the Big Boy Drive-in, where we went on Friday nights when my mother pleaded tiredness, and sat together, a hungry unit, as our Pontiac filled with the smell of toasted meat and onions and cigarette smoke. Occasionally, thinking of all the routes we never traveled, I'd suggest from the backseat that we try another way. And although my father might agree to this now and then, he usually forgot about it the next time, and there we'd be, crossing Allentown, leaving behind the square, fertilized lawns and entering, for a few blocks, someplace exotic.

I didn't mind, because I loved South Rosewood—the couples in cars, the screenless windows into which I hoped birds flew, the quality of music from a transistor fueled by a nine-volt battery, valiantly picking up a soul song all the way from Detroit.

It was after I started Marcus Aurelius that I realized that Mr. Jefferson was the head of one of these South Rosewood families. As we drove by, I began noticing him, illuminated by life—pushing a wheelbarrow around his backyard, or washing his car, or stepping out onto his stoop on Sundays in his shiny spats and pin-striped suit. He was a father, a landowner then, big-boned and real, and the first time I saw him like this I made my own father slow down so I could wave.

"Go on," my mother said after a minute, annoyed whenever my father obeyed me. "We're causing a scene."

Mr. Jefferson was getting into a black Coupe de Ville and looked blankly at us as I smiled from the backseat of our car. I was unsure why he wasn't responding—just that Friday he'd unlocked a storage cabinet for me and mopped up spilt milk right beside me in the school cafeteria.

My mother turned to me as my father sped up. "Who are you looking at, anyway?"

"Mr. Jefferson, our janitor, but he must not remember me."

My mother turned around with a sigh. "Why should he, Loretta. God."

In the estimation of our local world, janitors were down there with garbage men, although I didn't understand why. They all cleaned up our messes, and I thought we should be grateful. The women in my neighborhood drew their curtains on Tuesday mornings when the garbage men drove by, hanging rakishly off the back of the truck and jumping down at each yard. They wore gloves and laughed as they worked, amidst all our filth, that early in the morning. I was ashamed of the volume of our vast, privileged waste. Watching them carry away our bags, I agonized over the stale sweetrolls inside that I could have fed to the birds or been grateful for myself, over the plastic containers I could have washed out and put to good use, had I been industrious enough. I was sure that these laughing men could tell all about us from what we discarded, whether we pulled our curtains or not. And I wanted to tell that to the mothers around me and ask who they thought would ever be tempted by their pasty bulk.

Meeting these men in the street on my way to school, I began to regard them in an appreciative, respectful manner. And at Marcus Aurelius, I began holding the door open for Mr. Jefferson and his bucket, although he never actually looked at me when I did it or, I'm sure, understood why.

PART I

◆

Rosewood Avenue

Family Unhappiness

MY mother changed that year we moved to Rosewood Avenue, when she saw that my brother and
I were all she would accomplish in life. She became
convinced that her life had been cut short by marriage and that it was time to regret it, to view herself as a wasted resource, whether anyone else
recognized it or not.

She didn't have to say that we'd squelched her,
it came out in other ways—in migraines that sent
her to bed with a ravaged, twisted face; in spells of
melancholy, when she refused to take the meat loaf
from the oven, unplug the iron, or retrieve, let alone
open, the mail. If anyone asked her what was wrong
during these times, she would say that she never
got mail anyhow, that it was always addressed to
occupant or to my father, that she hated meat loaf
and would never cook it if she lived on her own,
that there was no reason to unplug the iron—was
there?—some part of my father's wardrobe for the
office always needed to be pressed. She said these
things, when she said them at all, to my grandmother, who was the only person who sincerely
attempted to find out what was wrong. She did not
like hearing these answers from my mother any more
than I liked overhearing them—they suggested
something rebellious about her, something mal-
functioning that I was afraid might explode, in
public.

She had her worst spells when she spent too much

time alone in the house, and on these occasions nothing would
occupy her for long. She'd begin to needlepoint pillowcases with
pastoral scenes, which I eventually found stuffed in the back of
our couch, a few halfhearted cross-stitches along the outline of
a pear or cow. She tried to buoy herself with projects for her own
self-improvement: learning Spanish by listening to 78 records
from the public library, or furniture upholstery from a craftstore
book. But day by day I could feel the steam go out of these
projects and notice that she progressively left them on some
pretense—to begin supper or wash her already clean hair, or
eventually, watch the black family who'd moved across the street
from us, the Terrells.

She grew fond of telling success stories of women who'd escaped
marriage entirely, especially Glenda Ball, one of her high-school
friends, who'd broken off a four-year engagement to a furniture
salesman in order to embark on a career as a court stenographer
in Cincinnati. Earlier on, when they were young, she and my
mother had taken trips to a lake in Indiana, where they wore lip
balm and tank suits and dreamed away the dank evenings with
what they would do with their lives. My mother was sure she
would be an interior decorator or a singer or blow her way to
stardom on her clarinet. In lieu of all this, she married my father,
although she and Glenda kept up a lively correspondence that
didn't end until the birth of my brother. But before that I was
privy to the most intimate details of Glenda's life, of how she
once bought a dozen angora sweaters in assorted shades because
she'd found a style she liked, of her vacations to spots near Bon-
ita Springs, Florida, where she stayed at the Sand Flea or the
Ocean Spray, charging it all to her expense account. My mother
offered as evidence of her carefree happiness certain Polaroid
snapshots Glenda included in her letters, but I thought she looked
just as lost as my mother, frumpish and baffled at the chlorine
pools, in her bermuda shorts and sunglasses. When Glenda disappeared, my mother took up with local women who were wid-

owed or divorced, and seemed more at home with their solitary woes than in the midst of young and cheerful mothers.

"Anyone can get married and have kids," she would say, and then invite me to look around us. Indeed, I only had to scan our neighborhood to find plenty of evidence of family unhappiness. Across the street, an old woman named Mrs. Kiley had lived in ancient despair since her husband's desertion in 1931; she detained the mailman each day with her pathetic conversation. She hobbled across the street on two canes whenever there was a minor accident or a siren, taking advantage of the gathering to ask the series of questions that had been piling up inside her all week. Next door to her, Jane and Harold Robb were raising two monstrous sons, Darin and Erin, who shot sparrows with slingshots and tortured their female dog. There was a rumor that after the prolonged birth of Darin, Jane had suffered a nervous breakdown. She rarely left the house, and then only to hang up her laundry, line after line of heavy denim pants stretched in the sullen shapes of her husband and sons. On Saturday nights when the Robbs hosted a square-dancing group, the boys were especially wild. I could see them moving in and out of the darkness with flashlights and matches, building small fires and occasionally causing some animal to let out a brief, heartrending cry.

On such nights I communicated across backyards with my new friend Nancy Emmett by a code that involved switching on and off our bedroom lights. On and off meant hello; on and off twice meant goodbye, even though we were often confused by the careless light switching of others in our houses. No visitors were allowed in Nancy Emmett's house because her mother was so private; she had a retarded son, Billy, who made up his own words, full of drool and a protracted eeee sound. By adolescence, he was so troubled that he was forced to stay inside his room. He pulled out his penis and watered the shrubs; he tried to kiss women on the lips, wetly; he begged to lie down on the grass with someone. He was eventually sent to the Garfield School, where he lived from then on, making houses of popsicle sticks and twisted yarn designs that you were supposed to hang on the wall.

"It's too bad," my mother commented, as if she knew something private about this kind of thing. "There's no one on earth they'll ever let him love."

On most days, I played alone, wandering to the back of the TV station across the street to rummage for reels of old commercials and public service announcements. When I was more bold, I peeked in the back window at a local talkshow, the "Coral Baker Program." On every birthday of my life I'd sat in Coral's birthday chair, where she urged me to report my age, my parent's name, and my birthday wish into her microphone. If I rushed home quickly, I could actually view myself on the air, but this thrill, like most, faded with age. The rest of Coral's show was uninspired and watched mostly by shut-ins or ironing mothers, such as my own. Her guests were the chairman of the March of Dimes or the secretary of the Park and Recreation Department. At noon a woman named Dot sang "O Solo Mio" or "Oklahoma," and then a local musician groaned a finale on the studio organ. The show lasted three hours, from eleven to two. I would sometimes see Coral pulling away in the late afternoon, looking rather exhausted in her company car. With her apricot wigs and double-knit suits, she was one of the few unmarried women in Union who lived on her own, of the same cut and girth as my physical education teacher, Miss Trois Martin, who blew a brass whistle as she made us do somersaults in a long, harrowing line. Although my mother thought their solitary lives heroic, I noticed she befriended neither one.

Next to the TV station, across from us, was the spook house, an abandoned duplex with peeling paint and a basement of swimming rats. The neighbors wanted it torn down, but the owner refused; he lived in Phoenix because of asthma, and didn't have to look at it anyhow. Since it had been empty for nearly ten years, no one thought it would ever again be occupied, but the summer after we came, the fatherless Terrells moved in. They were a quiet, soft-colored group with lilting names—Timmy, Tammy, and Tyrone—and the eldest son, who worked at the foundry, saluted bravely with hat in hand whenever neighbors drove by. But the neighbors did not wave back—they were cruising by in mild outrage that the Terrells had moved in at all.

Joe Briggs, a retired navy man, was especially incensed by their arrival and sent around the neighborhood a muddled petition that sat for many days on my father's glass-topped desk. It said, in part, "It's a well-known fact that the invasion of Negroes into a community reduces the value of homes and instigates crime, violence, and vermin." It was not clear what he hoped to gain by this petition, since the Terrells had already moved in and paid—some said in cash—for the house, but I was sickened to think that a word as ugly as *vermin* would ever be seen by their eyes.

The Terrells began immediate renovation of the house, painting the front a bright green and tending the neglected, weed-filled lawn. And the mother, a dreamy-eyed woman named Rose, was someone my mother should have admired. She worked as a singer at Palm Gardens, a black nightclub, and we could hear her thrilling voice calling out to her children, even when she was in the house: "Don't make me tell you again! You heard what I said! Don't worry me, now!" Since she worked nights, we saw her coming home in the morning just as we got up. I sometimes caught my mother standing at the window, watching Rose in her patent leather high heels and cocktail dresses, but as soon as my mother noticed me, she pretended to be doing something else. When the youngest Terrell boy, Timmy, began coming across the street to play with my brother, my mother went outside and swept the blacktop, making false, inquisitive conversation. "How long's your mom been singing? When's she cook if she works all night?"

But when she actually came upon Rose face to face, when

they met each other in the street, or hood to hood in their cars, she pretended not to see her, to be deeply preoccupied. Rose did not have to pretend; she had other things on her mind. With a cup of coffee in one hand and a cigarette in the other, she wandered out rarely, and then only to consult her older son or send the younger ones on errands; then she scanned the whole neighborhood in a tired, nonspecific way and walked up the rickety front steps slowly, as if her legs ached. My mother said it must have been those high heels.

As a newcomer, my mother was carefully neutral in her comments about the Terrells, but the rest of our neighborhood was united by their arrival. Nancy Emmett's mother opened up her house to host meetings of the Child Conservation League, a flagging organization that sprang to new life; the first meeting was called Another Look at Segregation. Mrs. Kiley struggled onto her breezeport, where she had a good westerly view of the Terrells, and detained the mailman more than ever with her fearful inquiries. Coral Baker replaced Dot's spunky show tunes with a weekly series called "The Melting Pot, 1961" and received outraged letters from shut-ins, who thought she was being too controversial. Darin and Erin Robb ceased tormenting animals and their mother long enough to commit acts of terrorism on the Terrells and their property; they threw cherry bombs in the front yard, drew chalk crosses on the asphalt, or simply stood watching, with their blank blue eyes. And Joe Briggs donned parts of his old navy uniform to head a Neighborhood Alert, in which he and several other husbands wandered the block, smoking Chesterfields, from nine to ten each night.

It was impossible to tell how the Terrells reacted to all this because Timmy, our main contact, was a quiet child. Sometimes I would spy on him and my brother while they played jacks or ball or war, as if I were viewing something monumental. But whenever Timmy moved out of the range of Rose's vision, whenever he slipped around to our backyard or into our garage, we would hear her voice calling out of the house: "Timmy Terrell, you come home now. That's enough."

I could see this was a hard time for my mother, who sensed the precarious morality of the situation we were in. When I asked if Tammy could come over and spend the night, she said she was getting another migraine and would let me know later, then spent the whole hot afternoon and evening in bed, with her door shut, which eventually answered my question clearly enough. I overheard her talking about Timmy to my brother in a low, hurried voice: "All I'm saying is you don't have to play with him every minute. And there's no reason for the two of you to come in the house." She seemed unusually tired that summer and vaguely ashamed of herself; she walked up the stairs to her room in the same slow, tired way I had observed in Rose. But she refused to join the Child Conservation League, saying the dues were too high, and called the Marcus Aurelius school about the treachery and truancy of the Robb boys.

At the same time, the Terrells began to retreat from us and only moved about at night in their dark late-model car. Timmy said he had homework whenever my brother asked him to play, and Tammy began to choose the company of dolls instead of me. Tyrone stopped painting the house midway, leaving it in two-tone stripes of green and white, and seemed disenchanted with mowing the lawn. Soon there was a For Sale sign.

Their house was eventually bought by a family of Christian Scientists, who vowed to gut it and fumigate. The wife, who introduced herself as Mrs. Devota Mann, clicked up and down our street in a jaunty, proprietary way, clutching her vinyl purse, as neighborhood women wandered to the hem of their yards to meet her. But my mother pulled our blinds as if one of us were ill.

We finally glimpsed the life of the Terrell's as they packed up to leave. For several dry, cool days their living quarters assembled on the lawn: a maroon couch with an oil spot where a man had once rested his head, a marble-based lamp, a frayed and magnificent rug—antique, my mother said.

The morning before their departure, she took out my old rose-colored Schwinn and wheeled it across the street to the Terrells. Months before I had asked if I could give it to Tammy, but she had not answered or had done so obliquely, saying we might fix it up one day or sell it to someone. I saw Rose open the screen door and my mother stand in the threshold, not entirely inside. They stood like this for several moments while I tried to imagine my mother's voice.

"Mrs. Terrell, I never fit into this neighborhood myself."

"My daughter's outgrown this bike, and we're all so fond of Tammy . . ."

"Dear Rose, can't we at least be friends before you go?"

But all I heard was "before we junk it" rise up like a skirt on the breeze.

The screen door slammed, and I saw my mother clumsily rolling the bike off the porch and down the walk. I couldn't see her face, or could not bear to look at it, but I saw Rose's dark hand yanking her only remaining curtain shut. My mother looked up at our house and must have seen me there, studying her and Rose and this time and place where we all found ourselves inexplicably stuck. Then, to my surprise, she mounted the bike and instead of wheeling up our driveway, took a sharp left and coasted down the hill, her hair fanned in the wind like the carefree girl she claimed she once was, the kind I was still supposed to be.

Castoffs

MY father insisted on donating our old clothes to the men's mission off Main Street instead of the Goodwill nearby. I didn't understand how the mission was helping these men, since each time we drove by they were lined up outside, no matter how cold the weather. Perhaps handing out cups of coffee and overcoats was considered enough, but my father didn't think so and grew solemn whenever we traveled this block.

For a town as small as ours, there was an oddly large representation of vagrants and prostitutes; the latter displayed themselves in front of Handlers, the appliance store a block from the men's mission, where my father held a part-time job. As you drove by, you could regard these women with the same consumer interest as the top-loading washers and electric heaters and vacuums that collected dust in the windows. In fact, they were one of the first sights to greet you when you pulled off the Main Street exit from Route 175: They stood in their matted fake furs in the winter, their pink hot pants in the sun. Their presence seemed a warning to the girls of Union that if they couldn't type fifty words per minute, or bear clerking at Woolworth's candy counter (next to the bird department, so that the ju-jus and chocolate-covered peanuts tasted of molt), or find a mild husband to prop themselves up, this might also be their lot.

Lou Handler, the owner of the appliance store,

had never seemed bothered by the existence of prostitutes; in fact, some people in town insinuated that he even welcomed it, to the point of occasionally inviting one into the perpetual evening of his navy-blue Ford. But during the second year my father worked there, Lou suddenly began to mind having them stand in front of his store, saying it cheapened his business.

He was a man who had come to late, blazing life after the death of his wife, a woman commemorated above his desk in a dreamy watercolor. Soon after her funeral, he took up with a deeply tanned, much younger woman named Miss Ruth Ellis, and began displaying behaviors never witnessed before. He escorted her to a dinner-dance club in Piqua, he bought her new whitewalls and handpicked teardrop earrings from Harts Jewelers downtown.

I knew about Miss Ellis because my mother used her as an example of what could happen if you spent too much time in the sun.

"It has a retroactive effect," she said, pleased to use a word that I probably wouldn't know. "All the time you've laid out adds up, and one day you have to face the consequences."

I hated this concept, as my mother must have known I would. I could accept immediate consequences—that a hand in a flame would hurt now seemed fair—but the notion of old acts bringing fresh costs appalled me, and I stared out the window with morbid fascination at the wizened head of Miss Ellis when Lou Handler brought her by our house.

But my mother's interest in Miss Ellis extended beyond her leathered face; this women's very existence in conjunction with Lou Handler incited her to outrage.

"In twenty years of marriage, he never bought his wife so much as a dishwasher. Now soon as she's in her grave, he's got Ruth Ellis dangling diamonds all over town."

"He's only bought her rhinestones so far," my father corrected;

he inevitably stuck up for Lou Handler after fueling my mother's outbursts.

"Rhinestones, diamonds, what difference does it make? You saw what Mrs. Handler had on in her casket—a sterling silver band and an old brass cross."

"He probably didn't want to bury good gold," my father said, rising from the kitchen table to make his escape. He, like me, enjoyed riling my mother, but didn't care to stick around for the consequences.

WHEN Lou Handler and Miss Ellis went to Acapulco the next month, he asked my father to take care of the prostitution problem.

"How'm I supposed to do that?" my father asked.

"I don't know. Call the police. Arrange something," he said.

My father was innocent in many ways, but not foolish enough to enlist the local police department, a group of young Union men who had found even junior high school taxing. So the Monday after Lou left, my father went out to the scraggly line of young women in front of Handler's and tried to talk with them himself.

This was hard for me to imagine when I heard about it later— that my father would consider himself persuasive enough, street-wise enough, to confront a group of women who had stood on this strip of concrete for years. It was hard for me to remember that my mild father was a salesman after all—a man who could convince couples of the virtues of an Amana spin-dry, and who, even more amazingly, sold insurance during the rest of his time, a service for which people received nothing concrete in return, only a numbered policy, and, he insisted, peace of mind.

When he returned home that night, he joined my mother and me in the kitchen and told us all about it. How he'd talked for fifteen minutes before one of the girls—Maria, he said her name was—suggested they go around the corner to DelWees and continue over lunch.

"You had lunch with a bunch of prostitutes?" My mother turned away from the kitchen mirror, where I'd been watching her mouth work away, and faced him with wet and shriveled hands.

"Well, I just had a sandwich. They were starved, I'll tell you. I had to order three or four rounds of fries."

"And you paid for all this, I bet."

"How much is lunch at DelWees?" My father shrugged, beginning to rise from his chair and leave us again.

He often wandered into deep water like this with my mother and, like a schoolboy, always seemed half surprised. My mother already disapproved of DelWees—a greasy spoon she called it—because of the derelicts from the men's mission who congregated at the counter all day, prolonging single servings of Post Toasties, which they ate straight from the box. But even worse, from my mother's point of view, my father insisted on talking to these men, who sometimes appeared in one of the threadbare suits he'd donated to the mission. This tickled my father—seeing a stranger walk in the door wearing his clothes—and he couldn't help but tell the man about it and where the suit had come from and what my father had once done in it. One man, named Dirk, still wore a much weathered version of my father's wedding trousers.

These men's sad tales did not move my mother. She did not like to hear that it was only because of a house fire that one man had become a tramp (my father liked this immensely, since it highlighted the importance of insurance). She did not wish to hear that another had once been an officer of an Upper Sandusky bank. That these bums were separated from our fate by small twists of bad luck—an unfortunate hunger for liquor, a gambler's penchant, a devastating divorce—infuriated, not softened her. But my father told her these stories anyway, guilelessly, time after time—as well as describing his lunch choice at DelWees, always something unhealthy she never would have served at home: a fried pork tenderloin sandwich, a double cheeseburger with hashbrowns, or his favorite, egg and bacon on white bread.

"So what was the outcome of all this?" my mother asked when my father headed toward the living room.

"Not much. They said they felt safe standing in front of the store, like nothing bad would happen to them."

"I don't know what worse can happen to you than becoming a prostitute," my mother replied, and then I left the room myself. This sounded not only cruel to me but somehow untrue.

WHEN Lou Handler and Miss Ellis returned from their trip and found the prostitutes still congregated in front of the store, he fired my father on the spot. This was the most shocking behavior he'd displayed so far, and my mother insisted that Miss Ellis had put him up to it, since she had a ne'er-do-well brother in Canton who wanted the job. But for whatever reason, my father, at forty, was fired from a job for the first time in his life. He took it as he took most hard things, with surprise, then confusion, then silence.

"That's the end of that," he remarked.

My mother, however, could not accept it so lightly, and harped frequently on the topic, especially to Joan Baxter, a woman on our street who had become sympathetic to surprise misfortune ever since her husband had been demoted from high-school principal to deliveryman because of a brain tumor.

"It's not that we need the money. It's the principle of the thing," my mother said into the receiver. "Bud's been doing all the dirty work for Lou Handler for years. Just last month he sent him out to talk to a bunch of prostitutes!"

As annoyed as I was by my mother's histrionics, I was upset myself. Hearing about my gentle, hardworking father being booted out of Handler's left a raw spot in my stomach, similar to how I felt on our last vacation when a tour guide at Ohio Caverns yelled at him for touching a stalactite.

MY mother insisted we take our castoffs to Goodwill after that. She associated the men's mission with DelWees, then Handler's, a twisted logic, but she pushed until my father-agreed. On one warm weekend she enlisted us both in cleaning the second floor of the house. We stood at the bottom of the attic window while she threw down items, but my father objected to nearly every one.

"That's my army coat! Those are books from business college!"

But the attic was insulated, and my mother had the transistor turned to WCID, where the announcer was telling her something she already knew—that it was going to be another overcast day.

We stuffed pillbox hats, wool suits, Candyland games into plastic bags, and had filled up five by the time my mother stuck her head out the window.

"OK, that's enough for now. I've got to start dinner."

We loaded the bags into the backseat of the car, and then my father got in and started the engine.

"You can come if you want," he said, watching me watch him.

I usually didn't want to go with either one of my parents; their journeys were so uninspiring. My mother made a regular path to the drugstore, the grocery, the dry cleaner; my father, as far as I knew, only went to his jobs. But what else was I going to do today, a white Saturday in March? I looked up and saw my mother regarding me with the flat look of a stranger, and I got into the car.

The trip should've taken ten minutes. Goodwill Industries was in our neighborhood, a low concrete building where the handicapped—another large population in Union—sat in their wheel-chairs, extended their hooked arms, and sorted through old clothes. But my father kept driving, past North Street, past Wayne. I didn't have to ask where he was heading, although I found it hard to believe.

He pulled up in front of the men's mission and unloaded four of the bags, leaving me in the idling car. I watched him stop beside one of the men who was sitting in the parking lot, leaning against a brick wall. He was an old man, entirely gray, until his mouth broke at whatever my father said to him, and I caught a glimpse of white and pink, teeth and gums—a smile.

"You forgot a bag," I said when my father returned, instead of saying all the other things on my mind, such as what was the men's mission ever going to do with a pillbox hat?

"That stuff's mine," my father said flatly, putting the car in gear.

When we slowed again, this time in front of the appliance store, I found that I was holding on to the door handle, as if he'd been driving recklessly. It was the first time I'd seen the prosti-tutes close up in the flat light of day, but they didn't look much more defeated to me than the housewives on our street. They gazed at us skeptically until the biggest one—a blonde wearing a blue dress and red tights—recognized my father. At a word from her, all three of them approached. When my father leaned over to roll down my window, I smelled the birthday present I always gave him: Old Spice lime cologne.

"Where you been, Mr. Dardio?" the blue-and-red woman asked.

"Had to move on," he replied simply. "Business got bad."

"Yeah, we're slow too," a dark one remarked. "Mr. Handler's girlfriend called the cops on us."

"Remember what I told you," my father said. "You got as much right to be here as anyone else."

The women were studying me, and I was surprised at how

much I liked their attention. But then my father seemed to remember my presence; he drew back and with a little honk our car began moving again.

"Miss seeing you, Mr. Dardio," the big one called after us.

WE drove home in silence then, the regular way, the way we would have gone had my mother been along. But the silence was unusual, though no one else would have noticed. It had electricity in it, like static on the radio. When we got home, my father remained outside as I walked into the house. My mother was on the telephone, the back of her head rimmed with rollers.

"You're telling me," she was saying to someone, probably Joan Baxter.

She didn't even turn around when I slammed the door, holding my father's plastic bag. That's how sure she was; that's how much she thought she knew then.

A Suicide

THE morning after Jim Willis killed himself, there was a photograph of us in the *Herald News*, standing huddled in wrappers and slippers from Rink's Bargain City, coordinated by our mothers in Easter pastels. At nine, I am posed in profile, glancing over my shoulder, listening for the siren heralding the county ambulance corps, who were, as usual, too late. Only the dullest, dimmest boys in town were ever recruited to their ranks—boys like Ricky Oswald, one of my classmates, who years later dropped my father from a stretcher during one of his coronaries.

But to be fair, the ambulance corps couldn't have come on time, because as the article that accompanied our photograph attested, Jim Willis had died instantly of a bullet wound at the roof of his mouth, that sensitive region I had often burned with cream of tomato soup, my mother's specialty. A coward, some might have said, for escaping so fast, but the effects of his sudden death lasted longer than anything he'd done in his vague and silent lifetime.

Our photograph appeared on the front page of the *Herald News*, parallel with a story about Khrushchev, but you could land in the *News* for fainting at the Elks during a tight night of poker, as my uncle had once done, or for driving around Speker's Breaded Veal without a proper muffler.

Marta Willis and her mother, Dortha, were obviously absent from the photograph and were only listed, with other survivors, as an afterword at the end of the article. Marta was older than I and not a best friend of mine, but in the casual way of neighbors, I knew her life. I had been in her room, for example, and lain on her bed—which was surely knowing someone however you looked at it. And it was this personal connection, this having entered the Willis's house often enough to recognize their distinct family scent, of having eaten a number of Dortha's bad granular oatmeal cookies, of having sat at ease on their rusty toilet a number of times, that made this event more than theirs, more a neighborhood suicide.

Jim I didn't know, but no one knew fathers. Even the best of them appeared only at dusk, shadows carrying empty lunch cartons, or on bright Saturday mornings, when they woke you up with their mowers and you felt an unnameable, unwarranted safety at that first scent of cut grass. But the worst of them were never seen, except for slamming in and out of cars, carrying six-packs of beer, or worse, with nothing, their red hands hanging dangerously empty at their sides.

Jim Willis, like my own father, fit neatly into neither of these categories. He was quiet and usually invisible, unless you took backyard routes that cut into his solitude; then you might see him looking out at his neglected lawn. We knew he was a father simply because he lived there, because people said so, not because he was actually seen sitting with his family on the couch. He looked at us girls in a hard way when we crossed his line of vision, as if he did not know who we were, that we had intimate daytime knowledge of his kitchen, his bath. To us, he was an altogether unremarkable man except for his marriage to Dortha, who was a cripple—a twisted, wincing woman—and we wondered, with the cruelty of girls already damned by ignorance and standards that would soon be used to diminish us, why he'd ever married her. Perhaps she had been stricken right before their wedding in some great, bloody accident, we conjectured, but that notion was dispelled by their wedding picture, which someone eventually saw, featuring Dortha leaning on a crutch, holding onto Jim's already withholding arm.

He was surely from Ohio; no one immigrated here, ever, and I understood why. There was no body of water nearby, for one thing. Oceans and rivers, for us, were scenic features for nature shows and greeting cards. We had only vacant lots and alleys, and, on the outskirts of town, fields of soybeans that smelled when they were processed, for what, we could not imagine. People only left our stagnant pond of a town; I had my own enigmatic plans for escape, shaped by Saturday-afternoon movies while my mother snored softly behind me on the couch. I did not know what would become of me, but whatever it was, I was sure it would not happen here.

Not like Jim Willis, whose beginning and end was so needlessly concentrated in this one dull spot. Couldn't he have driven his Ford across state lines to Fort Wayne and shot himself there? At least this would have caused some difficulty, a bit of speculative seasoning. But no; he merely plodded down to the basement, one much like ours, although a bit more messy. Dortha did not seem to have the coordination or inclination for the kind of robust neatness to which my mother subscribed. Even my father's nails, mostly rusty since he was never very handy, were jarred in old canisters, like grain, and labeled in my mother's tilted hand. In fact, I had not seen Dortha in more than two positions: one collapsed upon herself in an easy chair in front of the TV; the other propped up at the front door, looking out, usually at dusk, in a kind of anticipatory way. Perhaps she was sensing the future, sniffing at it, the way our dog lifted her head when my mother fried. Perhaps she knew that one day her husband would tromp down the basement steps in work boots and kill himself with a gun no one knew he had.

Surely she knew more than it seemed. Even if they did not

touch, she must have know something about a man she had
dreamed beside each night; some intimate knowledge must have
passed between them, if only through nightmares. My own parents called out frequently in their sleep, muttering warnings and
names that I woke to note, then quickly forgot. And my brother
often sleepwalked and peed in the linen closet. Certainly these
night facts were telling of something.

But Dortha told June Cooper, the bustling housewife who was
sent in as the neighborhood emissary that night, that she did not
know why he did it, did not know at all.

Who was Jim Willis anyhow? Food service, that was what
Marta answered when we asked about his job, as we sometimes
did in that idle way of girls, to construct a kind of hierarchy
among us. What this meant no one knew; it sounded as if he
were tending food with a rake or hoe, or pledging some kind of
allegiance to it, as Joe Briggs next door served the navy, with
much pomp and maximum use of his dress uniform, parts of which
he wore even when he accompanied his wife to the grocery. I
answered insurance, smugly, when someone asked me, although
in my secret heart I was none too proud of what my father was
doing to support us, which seemed to be scaring the wits out of
people over what might happen when they died. I was vaguely
aware that I was overly protected by a network of elaborate insurance policies, which meant there would be a neat profit for someone at my early demise and that I would be buried well, if there
was such a thing. I abhorred the idea of that, and the thought of
Jim Willis, sealed and bloodless below the ground at a depth I
might someday share, haunted me longer than his suicide.

Aside from Dortha, who took the event into her already injured
body with a mournful silence, it was the women of the neighborhood who seemed most affected by the death. They gathered
together more often in front yards for impromptu sessions, never
actually sitting down with coffee and cigarettes, as I thought grown

women ought to do, but with mail in their hands or clothespins in their mouths, always in the middle of something else.

"What could have been *that* bad?" I heard an especially naive one named Babs ask. It was a question I knew they considered from a personal standpoint, for they had their own silent and preoccupied husbands to contend with. The thought that it might not be enough—a plot of lawn, an easy chair, a wife, even a cripple, to greet each night—was a sobering one for our charmless mothers, who moved through their days as if on low voltage, doing what they'd been taught.

It was only we younger girls who admitted to the discontent that grew in us like the tumors our mothers whispered about— big as a pea, an apple, a grapefruit, we heard them say. Mine was already the size of a pea; Jim Willis's must have been the size of a grapefruit. Perhaps being in food service, he would have appreciated his woe being gauged by the very substance he once tended.

But something else happened the night of Jim Willis's suicide, apart from the fact that no event as monumental ever occurred in our neighborhood again. In the years that followed, the Michaels' house caught fire, but it was only a grease blaze in the kitchen, quickly contained. The Fetter girl became pregnant by a high-school dropout who skipped town at the news; Mrs. Kiley, our neighborhood old woman, had a stroke and was carried off to a warehouse where the elderly were stacked like spare parts of machines that were no longer in use. But all of this happened at dusk, behind closed blinds, accompanied by the soft click of car doors. Only the night of Jim Willis's suicide were we allowed out in our wrappers to watch.

And all we ever witnessed, eventually, was Jim's sheet-covered body, carried ineptly by the ambulance corps. Surely a fire would have been more visually dramatic, a mating more titillating, the twitching of a stroke more actively frightening. But our mothers had their wits about them on those other occasions and seemed to have lost them that night. When we heard the shot ring out, we looked for them to stop us as we put on our slippers and left our rooms, in the same way as pet dogs will hesitate, beckoning, before they shit on the rug. But they were fumbling too, with buttons and sashes, and moved out with us, equally unsure, into the dark. And for that moment, and that one only, we seemed united, nearly together.

Marta Miracle

I DID not know that Bobby Vee had two ee's on the end of his name until I got his autograph at the TV station. I went along with one of the older girls on my block, Marta Willis. By then I not only had my own autograph book but a turquoise autograph hound, signed eventually by a camp counselor, the minister's wife, and my grandmother: but Bobby Vee was my first and only celebrity.

He had one hit record I was aware of from listening to WCID on my transistor radio—a novelty then, tiny and Japanese and jacketed in the thinnest black leather. The song was "Run to Him," and Marta Willis grew dreamy over the lyrics as we sat out on old sheets in the front yard of yet another hot Ohio summer.

> If you find another who loves you more than I can love you, run to heeeuummmm.

I found this song, with its suggestion of multiple love that could be graded, then picked over like fruit at a market, astounding, and didn't like the false way Bobby Vee pulled out the last word at the end of each stanza. But Marta obviously appreciated what he was driving at and shivered appreciatively as we sat in her nest of movie magazines and hair-setting paraphernalia.

Everyone said I was too young to be hanging out with Marta, but since the death of her father I'd attached myself to her with a fierce protectiveness. Besides, I needed another female to listen to, because my own mother had grown silent, except for warnings. I liked to lie upon a bed that I'd never have to make, to go through Marta's drawers and closets, digging down through the intimate layers, stepping back through her blouses. I needed her because I was, among other things, sisterless.

It was possible that she allowed our friendship only because I was so agreeable and irrelevant, the way she didn't mind a stray cat hanging around. I was eleven to her fourteen, still young enough to have some interest in the outcome of a ballgame or dog fight. But Marta was past all that. She had entered the world of boys and men, and there didn't seem to be a moment, from when she rose each morning, her skull a complex arrangement of spit curls and spike rollers, that appealing wasn't on her mind. In fact, she left her hair up for two days and nights before we went for Bobby Vee's autograph; she wore the tightest red shorts she owned and the frostiest nail polish as we stood in a broken line of housewives and other teens to meet him.

Although he turned out to be plain and sandy-haired and average as a brother, Marta dug her glistening nails into my forearm as we shambled forward in line, autograph books in hand. My mind was already wandering to whether my mother would grill me cheese or pimento loaf for lunch, so I barely felt a thrill when Bobby smiled at me and signed *Luff Always* in my book.

To get further into her good graces, I let Marta borrow my autograph for the rest of the summer. It seemed to give her some obscure pleasure to have Bobby Vee's signature, in two versions, underneath her pillow each night, along with a napkin from a nightclub she claimed to have gone to with a high-school dropout, the bottle top from her first beer, and a length of pink ribbon that some boy or other had tied or untied or touched.

As desperately as I cultivated Marta, I couldn't help noting in my silent heart that she was often silly. I'd watched her defect into puberty like the other girls on my street: one day they were out tossing balls, scrambling through gravel; the next their tops were tucked in and they were slapping their thighs against the hot concrete on summer evenings—for exercise, they said. Girls my age appealed to them only as fools to be sent on errands. This had already happened to Marta and me.

"I'll give you a quarter to go over to Rice and see if Jim Carpenter is out playing ball," she'd wheedle, or, "You can listen to my Everly brothers if you'll call this number, ask for Jeff, and hang up if he's there." These and many other things I'd do for her, just so she'd continue letting me lie companionably on the bed where she tossed on her rollers all night, atop the talismans of her womanhood.

I planned to skip this stage myself, to grow, quick and clean, into a kind of woman I had never known. I would be the antithesis of everyone around me, even my beloved Marta, who now devoted whole summer days to her gigantic red hairdo, which she backcombed, sprayed, then protected with scarves before entering the world headfirst, as if she were balancing on her shoulders a precious, hollow orb. Although my mother was already chasing me around our yard with a hairbrush, I decided none of this would ever interest me.

But with all her preening and tossing, Marta had yet to be with a boy, until that summer of Bobby Vee, when she had her first encounter with one who followed her home in his car.

"It was so neat, Loretta," she told me as I lay draped across her bed. "He revved his engine behind me all the way down Allentown Road, but I pretended not to notice. Then he took off and drove around the block squealing his tires and came right up Rosewood. You should see him!"

I had seen him, from my second-story bedroom window, where I spent a good deal of time spying on our neighborhood. He was a boy of a certain menacing style—a pout on a blank face, a great swell of greased hair, a rusted, still powerful car that stunned cats and raccoons at night, then rolled over them, gladly. I knew he'd also been trailing girls on the other side of the block, but I didn't tell Marta this, knowing she would somehow blame me.

"What's his name?" She was teasing her hair again, preparing to meet him in an hour in front of the Delite Cafe, a location forbidden us both.

"Beau."

"Beau what?" I wanted to try on the idea of her forever lost to me, merged with this new and unworthy boy.

"Beau Miracle."

MARTA MIRACLE, I kept thinking all that night, a Friday, when we would usually be watching horror movies, screaming on her bed. At my house my parents were lost in an adventure show featuring gunfire, so I went up to my window post, feeling supremely neglected.

In the heat of the night, looking out at our blank street, my mind had nowhere useful to go. I thought of a Japanese boy in my class named Tim Ho and imagined names for his children—Gung and Westward and Hi—this was the kind of mood I was in. I must have dozed off with my head on the sill, because it was much later when Beau Miracle's car stopped across from our house, three down from Marta's, and the engine knocked off. Such a short distance would have never fooled my mother, but Marta's was not only a cripple but a recent widow who, having drank Pabst Blue Ribbon all day, went to bed early and slept deeply.

Out of Beau's Pontiac came a plume of cigarette smoke and a trickle of music, which had to have come from WCID, the only radio station transmitting that late. At this hour I knew that the disc jockey, Henry Clay, put on long-playing romantic albums so that he could finish his agriculture-school homework.

Beau's dark head was lost in the car interior, but I could follow

the regular movements of Marta's mammoth head. My heart beat
strongly as I watched it move back and forth, to and fro. When
it finally disappeared entirely, I felt a strong, sweet, perverse pain
in my torso.

It suddenly shot through me that Beau Miracle might be killing her, inserting into her tender flesh a switchblade, or worse,
and that there was no one left in the world to save her but me. I
left my post and ran down to our front yard, where I stopped by
the garbage cans, afraid to proceed.

The car was rocking slightly like a docked boat, then one of
Marta's feet appeared, shoeless, at the top of the front seat. It
was that hoof, pink as a pig's foot, that made me lose my reserve.
I picked up two garbage can lids and banged them together like
cymbals, and cried, "Marta Willis, get home!"

Then I dropped the lids and ran into the house and reached
my perch just in time to see Marta and Beau sit up as lights
flickered on in a lovely, almost orchestrated way in nearly every
house on our block. Women opened their curtains to press their
faces against their screens, and fathers walked out onto stoops in
their bathrobes.

Beau Miracle started his car as Marta, her hair mashed to one
side, was expelled from the Pontiac, her skirt twisted, her blouse
unbuttoned. Even from my window, I felt her hot gaze.

I never found out exactly what happened that night, because
Marta basically refused to speak to me, except to ask that I please
pick up my things from her room the next day. When she opened
the door, I saw that she sported a hickey at the base of her throat
It looked hot and painful, but she kept touching it, as if it were
a jewel.

"Your stuff's there," she announced.

Arranged on her bed was a Millie the Model comic book she'd
borrowed once, two conch shells I'd given her, a hairbrush, and
my autograph book. I felt a lump in my throat, at the same spot
as her hickey, when I gathered up my things and took what I

knew was my last look around her room before she banged the door shut behind me.

EVENTUALLY Beau Miracle cruised off, and Marta forgave me, but she still married younger than anyone in order to escape her mother's house. I'd occasionally see her when I came home from college, at neighborhood barbecues, where families spilled over the boundaries of yards and mingled, almost in spite of themselves. She'd grown wide of the hip and soft of the jaw, but her eyes still held a soft, green, intimate light when she spotted me.

I seemed to be more humorous to her in memory than I'd ever been in real life. I'd come upon her laughing, a freckled baby on her hip or hanging round her neck, and be amazed to find out that I was the object of the story she was telling. Her favorite tale was one the neighborhood women already knew, but Marta told it anyway, weeping with laughter when she got to the part about the cymbals.

"My hero! She thought she'd rescue me!"

Although I had not married, I was hardly a virgin, nor as unlike Marta as I'd planned. I wore a bra and shoes that hurt me and held a hand mirror some evenings and looked at the back of my head.

Knowing this, the neighborhood women turned to me, waiting for me to spurn my old and foolish ways. But I could only manage a smile, and a weak one at that, unable to tell them that night was one of the few when I'd known exactly what I was doing, and that I still regretted not saving Marta Willis, or myself.

Westgate Lanes

WHEN my mother began bowling, I was surprised on a number of counts. Westgate Lanes had always been a forbidden landmark of my childhood, semi-attached as it was to a bar where types quite unaffiliated with sport gathered to blow smoke over each other's heads and drink cheap and fragrant American beer. I knew this because I'd been blasted often enough by the tainted air that floated from the exit, where I stood in defiance of my mother, watching people depart. Inside were the drivers of big rigs that frightened my female relatives on rural roads late at night, men with arms roped by muscle, heads set with bright, rheumy eyes. Their women tried hard to look fragile, dyeing their hair a silvery ash that closely matched their skin—or what could be seen of their real skin—at their ankles and ears. But their faces had been worked over with smears of coral and mauve that were not rubbed in at the neck—a friend of mine claimed these were called demarcation lines—and their slacks were so tight that they could only perch halfway on stools or lean against the bar. My grandmother had already informed me that such tight garments smashed the intestines, and each time one of these women passed me by, I thought of her long, dark organs, twisted and twined like that, all for some elusive purpose of seduction.

These couples weren't married; at least they wore no rings, and when they left the bar, it was not in the matrimonial way I'd long observed: the man walking ahead, busy with his billfold, the woman behind, occupied with her headscarf, barely on the same trajectory, not expecting talk. No, when one of these couples left, the woman was tightly pressed to the man's side as they tried to move as a unit; he invariably slipped a hand, clever as a spade, into a tight back pocket or waistband. The woman left her battered sedan in the parking lot and leapt into the cab of a big rig, to be transported, presumably, to one of our town's seedy hotels.

I believed this was where they went chiefly because of how the woman looked when she was dropped off; sometimes in an hour, often the next day before lunch. Men did not seem as full of evidence to me then, but a passionate night on a bad mattress showed up on a woman in the bright of day; surely she did not have the resources to repair herself in a dim hotel mirror.

I watched the couples separate and the woman walk, without a kiss or endearment, to her car. Sometimes one of them would sit smoking a cigarette, as if gathering her wits, while the man pulled out of the lot enthusiastically, leaving behind a trail of exhaust and dust.

I had learned most of what I knew at that time about men and women from my observations in the bowling-alley lot, and I understood why my mother had forbidden me to go there. The view of the sexes she thought I should learn was the chaste and dull world of marriage, which involved, as far as I could tell, sitting down. This was what my parents did together, and my grandparents, and the other couples around us. They sat on the porch after dinner, in front of the television before bed; they sat in the front seats of cars, the women passive as cows while the men squinted and maneuvered, pretending that they knew exactly where they were going.

But in the bowling-alley lot, men and women did other things. There were fights, where the women stamped the delicate stilts of their high heels in the gravel and made demands—I did not know exactly what. They pulled away; they tossed their pale hair and cried out. What I witnessed there suggested a darker, more intricate reality.

Because there was nothing much for me to do in our town during the summer—no pool, only an x-rated cinema and one store downtown—hanging out in that expanse of gravel with such a show to observe was as illuminating a way as there was to spend a day. I liked being away from our house in the sun. I liked to sit in that parking lot as the light hit the hoods of cars, the expanse of cracked rock. I was still young enough to have the sense that I was part of what was green and growing on the land; I could almost feel myself swell with what I watched, when I watched it in sunlight.

Ironically, it was this exact lack of local opportunity that also drove my mother to the alley. I had thought her immune to boredom, but that summer of 1962, long and bright and hot as it was, had prompted some enzyme in her, some secretion or chemical, to change, and she announced to my surprise that she had joined the Methodist women's bowling team, sponsored by Clyde Ewan's Market, and that if I wanted I could join her for the games.

The shirts of the team were grass-green, with CLYDE sewn on in red thread. It was odd seeing my mother dressed so brightly, with a man's name scrawled across her back. I was skeptical in the first place about the Methodists sponsoring such a group; surely they had better things to do—feeding hungry people, for example, or praying somewhere.

"Everyone needs their recreation," my mother said smartly, a view that seemed to have bubbled up out of nowhere.

She did not seem hindered by the fact that she had never bowled, had probably never even witnessed a serious game. Following her lead, we walked into the alley that first day as if we belonged there, she carrying a vinyl bowling bag that contained gloves, a pair of shoes, and, best of all, her ruby-toned ball. She'd let me hold it in my lap the night she'd brought it home from the sporting-goods store.

"It's a deluxe model," she'd said, and along with the thrill of having that red, heavy weight rest between my legs, I also felt a certain anxiety that my prudent, previously homebound mother was being so extravagant.

Everyone else had a black ball, I noted with pride, and many were even using the dull, chipped ones that came with the alley. As we settled ourselves with my mother's team—four women with vaguely familiar faces and the same wide, lazy-looking behinds—I got a brief glimpse of the bar in the distance, almost empty at this early hour.

It was a long morning. After I'd situated myself at the score table for several minutes and watched my mother throw a number of gutter balls, I was already bored. Although she explained the purpose of the game to me, I couldn't understand the point— the big point—of why they would come, dressed like this, to knock down pins at all.

"It's a game," she hissed when I grumbled. Then she toddled off again for another miserable performance, which was much critiqued by the others; among other things, she twisted her wrist when she threw and repeatedly stepped over the starting line. Still, she was the only one who seemed serious about the game, despite her amateur status. The other women chatted merrily and smoked cigarettes, sometimes forgetting their turns entirely. Although my mother and I had agreed early on that I would learn to be the scorekeeper, the rest of the team's obvious lack of interest, along with my mother's repeated gutter balls, quickly dispelled the sense of importance I'd felt that morning.

For a time I managed to be curious about how the pins were picked up when one of the bowlers actually managed to knock them down. "It's automatic," my mother answered dully, but I meant exactly how—I wanted to climb in the cavernous area at the back and look.

"You can't," she said, a reflexive answer by then.

After an hour my mother's lack of success took a toll on even her enthusiasm. To make it worse, she was not good at mixing in public and seemed always to be joining the group and interrupting just as they were in the middle of some complex tale.

"What are you talking about?" she would ask, and the woman speaking would purse chagrined lips before she stopped and quickly recapped, my mother having ruined her momentum.

It embarrassed me to be witness to my mother's multiple failures. She finally gave me a dollar bill—a lot for her—so that I could buy some treat and, I knew, get lost.

"Stay away from that bar," she called out as an afterthought.

I spent some time in the ladies' bathroom, with its strong disinfectant smell and false light, studying my face, which looked unfamiliar here out in the world; I was only used to seeing it in the normal, homey light of our bathroom. Then I turned to the vending machines, which offered for a quarter an assortment of unnecessary items I could not understand why anyone would ever buy: floral rainhats, vials of perfume, vinyl carrying cases for the sanitary napkins that my mother had told me, warningly, that I would shortly have to wear.

The only thing I could think to do after that was to go into a stall, then burst out quickly in order to catch a candid view of myself in the mirror. This was a shock—I barely knew myself, so quickly, in such fluorescence. I did it several times until a cleaning lady appeared and gave me a sharp look. After that I walked to the snack bar and bought popcorn, but it was coated with a cold film of butter and tasted unnatural so early in the day. Then, after a quick check to make sure my mother hadn't followed me, I headed toward the bar.

It was walled off from the rest of the alley only by a pane of frosted glass, so I could stand at either of the two open entrances and observe easily while remaining outside. There were four people there: two women of the type I had often observed, sitting at a table, mostly silent, but sometimes laughing listlessly as if over bad jokes that were at their own expense. They looked once, rather hopefully, at the two men at the bar surrounded by cigarette smoke, once censoriously at me, but there seemed little potential for action.

"I'm just killing time," the blondest of the two women said.

Hearing such words inside a place that had so long occupied my imagination was a large disappointment. I saw that the lives of men and women, even here, were often slow and uneventful. I wandered from entrance to entrance until the cleaning lady, now finished with the bathroom and clanging her pail, stopped in front of me and asked, "Who do you belong to?"

Afterwards, I thought of many brilliant comebacks to this question, but being slow on my feet, I could only stammer, feeling the truth of it all at once, "No one."

"Well, minors aren't allowed in here," she snapped, barging into the bar with her can of filth and rags, breaking the reverie of the two women, who winced at her sound, surely from hangovers.

I headed back toward the Methodist team, but stopped at the shoe rental, not wanting to actually join them. My mother stood in profile, hopefully watching the journey of her ball. Only a daughter—or a fool—would have held her breath the way I did as it veered back into the gutter.

Square Meals

BILLY CAVIN had the pale curls of a sheep and the matted lashes of the very blond. His looks were from his father, a fine-boned man with the same white hair, who was a milkman for Sealtest. He left us chunks of butter, and squat bottles of milk that froze in the winter, soured in the sun. Despite this, my mother continued buying from him long after she'd gotten rid of the Jewel Tea man, who'd once tried to proposition her with a free set of brushes, and the Nickles Bread man, who had even stooped to plying me with warm, miniature loaves after we'd canceled because of finding a dead mouse draped across the cherry preserves of our breakfast rolls.

Although pragmatic in most ways, my mother had a soft spot for the meek and pale and silent, and had gone as far as marrying my father, possibly for these very reasons. But he had not only darkened with age but grown more churlish and vocal, and I saw how she might be able to harbor illusions about Mr. Cavin, blond and grave as he was in the early morning light, that were no longer possible with my very real father. She certainly wondered aloud often enough why Mr. Cavin had married his wife, who was known as a gossip, and a pious one at that. Not that my mother disapproved of religion; we went to church dutifully, if sullenly, each Sunday, looking as good as we could manage, to sit through the preacher's sermon as if enduring a punishment. But Mrs. Cavin was always there. She exploded, sweaty and aproned, from the kitchen at each pancake supper; she was the one who told you where to sit at mother-daughter banquets, the one who scurried about, her mouth full of straight pins, making last-minute alterations on choir robes or bridal gowns. All of this was excessive, according to my mother, who, showing an uncharacteristic interest in the subject of family, was sure that in the midst of such activity Mrs. Cavin was being neglectful.

"Look how pale Billy is," she said to me often, and indeed from watching him in our school cafeteria I had made several observations: that he only ate white things—potatoes, milk, eggs, hominy—and that he could not swallow a pill unless it was mashed in a spoon with jelly. I did not tell my mother these things; surely she would see them as evidence of something.

In fact, I tried to tell her as little as possible that year, feeling that something was quite definitely wrong. On her last birthday—her thirty-fifth—she had refused to let my father take her to the local steak house, as was his custom, and she secretly returned the saucepan set he gave her instead. And there were outbursts, different from her complaining, which by then was chronic. She wept protractedly when my grandmother's pomeranian, Fluffy, died a completely natural death; she also cried when I got a C instead of a B in history, and for no apparent reason, all one Easter. My father would look at me during these episodes with an exasperated complicity I did not like. He worked more and more, it seemed, as if to avoid her troubling presence. Sometimes I was actually shocked to see him walk into the house.

And her sigh! It swept through our house like some trade wind that year, prompted by anything. I knew things were bad when I heard it as soon as she sat up in bed. I thought that first acts—or sounds—were telling, that you were in trouble if you drank in the morning or smoked straightaway. To sigh like that, surely it meant she was yearning for something, but for what I did not know and was afraid to imagine.

But I had no idea how seriously occupied my mother's imagination was with the Cavins until one morning when I found her dressed in the red mules that she usually saved for Christmas morning. She stood at the door—one foot poked pertly out into the chilly morning—inviting Mr. Cavin and Billy over for supper. When she turned back into the house, the front of her had pinkened, either from the cold or excitement, and she quickly altered her unusually happy expression when she saw I was there.

"Mrs. Cavin's been called away to nurse her sick mother," she said in a voice that she usually reserved for explanations to adults. "I thought it would be nice to have them here."

I did not think it was up to me to point out that this was also one of the evenings when my mother and I would be alone—my brother was going to a Little League game and my father to a stag party at the Elks, an event my mother managed still to disapprove of, although he had been attending for years. In fact, this biweekly event was one of the major bones of contention in their marriage.

"I work all week," my father boomed when she brought it up. "I've got a right to enjoy myself."

"You should stay home on weekends and enjoy your family."

"I'm home all week. What do we enjoy?"

"That's my fault, I guess."

"You're the one who moons around all day. Think of something for us to do."

But in the end, my mother could think of nothing for us, and the accusation of mooning, as predictable as it was, always ended their discussion, and she would revert to slamming a door and carrying on anything more forceful she wanted to say from behind it.

"Stay out all night with those wastrel Elks, for all I care."

MY father did occasionally stay out all night after one of these outbursts, and I recalled now, as my mother shut the door behind Mr. Cavin, that they'd had a particularly rough exchange the night before and that he might stay away again.

I did not take sides in these arguments, although my mother assumed that, being female, I was loyal to her. But I understood my father's wanting to escape the terrible monotony of our living room, the clack of my mother's knitting needles, those low, oppressive, predictable nights. I could understand how he might have tired of the way my mother never spoke except to complain; the lull of the evening had the effect of ushering forth from her the report of anything wrong: her joints ached, the house was cold, the TV show that we were watching, and would continue watching, was dumb. But she didn't seem to expect us to try to rectify any of this, and made no move to do so herself.

On the other hand, she hardly mooned around, as my father suggested. I was witness to her endless bending and mending and scrubbing when I rushed through the house after school, hoping not to be nabbed to help. When I'd first started junior high, she had briefly greeted me with a glass of milk and a plate of snacks, asking me to sit down and tell her the events of my day. She must have read about doing this in some women's magazine, but she quickly gave it up when my reports suggested what an unremarkable student—person—I was. The day blanked out in front of me, empty as a chalkboard, when she asked me to describe it; the details I managed to rake together—the filling of my lunchtime sandwich, the hour of a fire drill—were clearly not what she had in mind. I wondered why she expected me to be able to do this—describe things, to use words like that—when I could barely remember her doing it herself. Even so, she was no mooner, or at least I had never thought so until I'd seen her turn away from Mr. Cavin with her unfamiliar smile.

MY mother cooked away the bulk of that Saturday the Cavins were coming. She was normally not a very industrious cook—more full of ideas than steam. This was one of the many skills she had not inherited from my grandmother, who was able to make a gravy from a single dripping, to cut perfect strips of homemade noodles with her pinking shears. My mother was usually too impatient for this kind of thing, knowing my father, brother, and me to be fast, unappreciative eaters who were up from the table and belching just as she settled down. Still, she did believe in the restorative effects of food, and if she didn't cook well, she at least cooked amply, always preparing too much, which gave her an excuse to stand in the kitchen later, picking the pans with her fingers. During the last year, I had discovered that she sometimes did this in the middle of the night; she scared me the first time I found her illuminated by the cool white glow of the refrigerator, eating leftover spaghetti and green beans from bowls with her hands.

All day our house, just shut up for autumn, was thick with conflicting aromas. Food seemed alive to me then, and from my room where I lay, already anxious at the prospect of entertaining Billy Cavin and his desirable father on my own turf, I thought I could hear the pork roast spit and moan from the oven, the potatoes collapse, defeated, under my mother's whirling blade, the last corn, surely bitter by now, wrenched from warm husks.

My mother had dirtied every pan by the late afternoon when she left the kitchen and sequestered herself in the bathroom, locking the door for the first time I could remember. My father had always been the one who spent a long time on an elaborate toilette, making it into a ritual of hot towels and foam, then bracing liquids and talc. My mother usually cleaned herself in the same brisk way as she scoured the toilet bowl, then drew on, at the most, a pale tangerine mouth.

But that afternoon the aroma of bath salts seeped under the door; I smelled cream rinse and mouthwash; I heard the fumble of the more exotic tubes and wands that she stored in a canister under the sink. When I was too full of urine and dread to wait any longer, I knocked on the door timidly, feeling I had been displaced in my own house.

"Yes?" she called out in a new voice, as if I could have been anyone else.

"It's me. I've got to go," I said, steeling myself, but it was worse than I could have dreamed. There was my serviceable mother—the workhorse, the complainer—with sea-green eyelids, a fresh mulberry mouth that glistened invitingly, and a new elevated hairstyle, achieved I could not imagine how. Seeing her like that was one of the greatest shocks of my short life.

She removed her paraphernalia from the toilet stool, watching me all the while, as I dropped my drawers and sat down, feeling that I was peeing out a gallon of unhappiness.

"You have to get ready soon yourself," she said to me finally.

"Ready for what? They're only coming to eat."

"You sound like your father," she replied, turning back to the mirror to complete a half-finished brow. She looked back at me when she was finished, and the effect of the new arc made her look indecently surprised. "Sometimes you should just *try*."

I DON'T know how I made it through that evening. Both Billy and his father were clearly taken aback by my mother's spread, as elaborate as for a holiday, by her festive apron and bright lips, by the clickity-clack of her high heels as she dashed unnecessarily in and out of the kitchen—I hoped she was going back there to calm down. I could not meet Billy's matted eyes and wondered desperately how I could ever face him again in school. But I managed to covertly study Mr. Cavin and was able to remove myself enough from the situation to see why my mother found him attractive. Out of his dull uniform, he looked as if he came from somewhere else—somewhere far, like England, or an even farther place that I could not yet name or know. I imagined him briefly in heather fields, with sheep, a muffler about his neck.

My mother kept up the most animated conversation I had ever been witness to, bursting out of the kitchen with a new question to pose to Mr. Cavin, smiling intently each time he elaborated his reply. Who would have ever known that she had an interest in local politics, the sewage-treatment plant, the management of Sealtest? Not I; not she, probably. I saw that one of the things women were supposed to be good at was manufacturing interest, right out of thin air, and thought dully that at some point I would probably be expected to do the same.

But Mr. Cavin, for all his outer charm, did not manage to ask much of my mother. That would have cinched it in my book— if, along with his continental looks, he had actually been interested in her. But in his defense, what could he have asked her? Her brand of floor wax, how she had managed to elevate her hair so drastically, where my father was this night? That was a question I felt beating in the air anyway; absent spouses, glinting wedding rings, seemed to roam the room like ghosts. It seemed to me that Mr. Cavin would have had to delve deeply into my mother's past to find anything of interest, back to her old hopes— to play the clarinet in an orchestra, to take voice lessons, her brief and inexplicable desire to travel to Maine. These were the only possible areas of interest, and surely this route was too intimate for such a meal.

When toward the end of our dinner my mother experienced a wane in her inquisitiveness, Mr. Cavin filled in the silence by exclaiming in a methodical way about everything he had eaten, which I imagined in mass, churning away in his delicate stomach.

"Your mother's usually too busy to prepare a big meal like this, right, Bill?" he asked, clapping the boy affectionately on the back.

Billy nodded, while my mother brightened.

"I always manage to serve my family three square meals," she said.

"Not that our meals aren't square," Mr. Cavin said quickly. "We eat well enough. It's just that my wife's usually got better things to do than cook all day."

The charged atmosphere of the evening seemed to leak from the room as Mr. Cavin proudly listed everything his wife did out in the world. We had always imagined her rooted in church, full of sweat and gossip. But no—she volunteered at the old-folks home, at the hospital, she drove the handicapped around.

We heard stories of her ingenuity, her courage and resourcefulness. We heard how good she was in an emergency; once she'd even put out a grease fire by herself. I reddened as I listened to him, feeling that he was defending his wife, in her absence, against an evening that had been designed to denigrate her. I could not look at my mother; I knew she was silently measuring her own absorbed, narrow life against the accomplishments of this wide, appreciated woman.

My mother finally excused herself to go back out to the kitchen, where she stayed a long while, leaving me in an agony at the table. When there was a loud bang, I ran in to find that she had dropped the gravy pan and splattered pork grease all over the front of her good wool dress. I do not think I have ever seen her look so sad: her mulberry lipstick had been eaten away; her hair looked wilted, tamped down. The only thing I could find to be glad about was that there was no mirror around.

In silence, I helped her clean up the mess, praying she would not start crying, then realizing that this was too typical a situation—her tears were only exotic, unexpected.

"Everything all right in there?" Mr. Cavin called out, and when my mother didn't answer, I stuck my head into the dining room, where they still sat, rooted, like two wooden soldiers.

"Fine," I lied, wishing they'd simply leave.

I saw my mother had apparently returned to her senses, since she did not rush off to change her dress. She walked back out, the grease stain ranging not only across her breasts but also over the area spanned by her girdle.

"Looks like we've had an accident," Mr. Cavin said, more charming than ever now that it no longer mattered.

"Yes," my mother said vaguely, but she did not look at him; her face had rearranged itself into its normal look of passive pain.

Mr. Cavin must have seen this, for he thanked my mother again quite effusively and then quickly ushered Billy, who had not uttered a word all evening, out our front door, forfeiting an angel food cake, which still sat like a hat on the table.

"Would you clean up?" my mother asked as soon as they were gone, the second time that day she had addressed me as an adult.

I nodded as she headed for the bathroom, where she shut, but to my great relief did not lock, the door. As I cleared off the table, I imagined her wiping the green paint from her eyelids, kicking off those painful pumps. And when I positioned myself in front of the kitchen sink, I felt her turn off the bathroom faucet at the same moment I turned mine on, and thought that in this house without words, perhaps, in this way, we were communicating somehow.

In the Country

BECAUSE I was so young when he died, I hardly knew my father's father. He died in the country, in the same abrupt manner as he'd lived—simply closed his eyes one morning and let his old heart stop. But I had a late view of him, according to my mother, who had taken along with my father's name a proprietary interest in the Dardios, as if they were somehow, through marriage, much more hers than his. This did not mean she loved them, as much as she thought she knew them, and in her middle years, when she had run out of toddlers to thwart and part-time jobs that drained off, like cream, the top layer of her nervous energy, she took to researching in great detail my father's family tree. She became his archivist, in a way.

It was not an enterprise for which I could muster much enthusiasm, mostly because the women on these diagrammed sheets seemed only to have been born, married, and died. Sometimes their maiden names were lost for good, but this did not seem to bother my mother, who charted the endeavors of the lost men in my father's family with a zeal I found suspicious.

She had her own family, of course, who were less scattered and who we saw more often, but she was as curiously detached from them as I would be at the family gatherings she later orchestrated herself.

"Nothing's ever new here," she sighed as she sat

apart at barbecues and birthdays, listlessly eating the three-bean salads and jello molds that constituted the extent of her own culinary imagination. She seemed to be implying that if it weren't for bonds of blood, she would have never chosen to know these people, her family, at all.

I didn't think she would have chosen my father's family either, but she had certainly chosen my father, with his background of thrift and silence. There had been many older siblings, mostly sisters, on his side of the family, but a number had died long ago, some through difficult-sounding illnesses, like diphtheria, others by that most trying act of all—being born. My father's remaining sisters were scattered through marriage by the time I could know them, in regions of the country I could not even locate on a map. And when they did show up yearly at family reunions, in tandem with their husbands, who were in the navy or held vague jobs at National Cash Register or GE, they were so reduced by marriage and motherhood, so sunken into themselves that I could hardly locate the family features that stood out so distinctly in the few sepia photographs my mother had gathered of my father's family.

My father was a struggling insurance salesman for Mutual of Omaha by the time his father died, and he seemed curiously detached from any roots other than the rather shallow ones we were all feebly putting down right then.

"He doesn't have time for things like that," my mother said, reporting on him as if we weren't all living together in the same house.

I could see for myself how the world of business—the nights of adding machines and cigarettes, the jostling for accounts— was taking an extraordinary toll on my father, who seemed just barely himself. Even on Saturdays, after his breakfast of glazed donuts, he went immediately to the Elks for poker, as if he could not bear for a moment to be without the company of men, amidst the air of futile competition.

But we have him on days like this one—a Sunday, when my mother manages to intimidate us all into attending church, although once there, her mind is more on the upcoming dinner than the words of warning and doom that register plainly on my father and settle through me slowly, like some time-released drug, all throughout the day.

We have him for our heavy Sunday meal, which has simmered on low throughout the services, the entire dinner in a black speckled roaster, so that the roast beef and carrots and potatoes cook into each other in a disconcerting way, and look exhausted, defeated by the time they reach our plates. Having overeaten, my father snores in front of the dreadful shows that air on Sunday afternoon TV, shows that seem to be presented as some sort of punishment for our expecting entertainment on a holy day. My brother and I lie on the floor in front of my darning mother while we watch Oral Roberts cry over the blind and lame and hearing disabled, clucking with her skeptically when hearing aids and crutches are thrown through the air as he cries, "Thank Jesus! You're saved." We watch "Industry on Parade," a great, dull program that takes you inside automated dairy plants and steel foundries, revealing a dark, mechanized world that no one really wants to learn about. This is followed, just as my father is about to wake, with "High-School Quiz," where genius boys from Indiana spew out facts about physics and astronomy that none of us will know, ever.

I am more disconcerted on these flat Sunday afternoons by this show than any of the others. I want to be quick and full of numbers; if not, I at least want to be active, not lying about in a great herd with my family. My mother, by this third hour of television, has put down her darning and is watching my father doze.

"He's getting to be just like his dad," she says in the explanatory tone that guides use to describe objects in museums. Then she wakes him: "Bud . . . come on. It's time to take us for a ride." This seems to be our due, this Sunday afternoon ride, which my father has to preside over, although my mother has a valid Ohio driver's license in her neat billfold and can take us any-where with perfect legality and ease. But we wait for him; he emerges from sleep with a boyish look that disappears when this waning Sunday, my mother's expectant face, the world of work and worry finally rise up again in his consciousness.

WE never drive anywhere new on these rides, just out of town via back roads that cut across soybean and corn fields, past a creek we fished in long ago when my father still had time. He is in a good mood once we reach the country, and he honks at any lone man we see. "Hey there, Charlie!" he calls out, and the man nearly always waves back. This anonymous greeting thrills me, as if there is a great goodwill out in the world waiting to be tapped; as if anyone we want to know is just there, ready for us, only needing to be honked to, waved at.

During this ride, as on many others when my mother is tired or silent, memories of childhood dribble from my father, like a mouthful of scalding tea. He talks often of his mother, whose legs were amputated the year she died. "Even then she mopped the floor every day from her wheelchair," he says. He talks of what she did without, the deaths of children she endured with-out complaint. She seems mythical to me, saintly in her silent strength, and as my father speaks, he lets the car veer to the median in the sorrow of remembering her. This is enough to jolt my mother out of her reverie, and she navigates him back into the safety of the suburbs, to streets where she can note curtains and lawn furniture and petunia arrangements she might mimic later on. And just as surely she steers his memories toward the men of his family, those traveling begetters whose lives she has so charted on her tree: "Why don't you tell that story about your old Uncle Jake."

My father does, and I listen as we let her take us back to our world, away from what we are drawn to and scared of—that green region of feeling that opens up like a silent lake whenever we drive into the country.

Miniskirts

WHEN a man who grew up in our county orbited the earth, my mother wasn't impressed.

"Might as well waste money here, if they have it to waste," she said.

Her cousin, Patsy Long, disagreed, as she almost always did with my mother. "We're witnessing a new era," she said to her daughters with dew in her eyes.

Patsy Long dyed her hair the same soft pink blond as her face and favored birthstones welded onto clustered rings that stood out garishly when her hands worked on raw meat or submerged in bleach water. She could be explained, as she often was, apologetically, by my grandmother, by the fact that she'd been neglected by a widowed mother who'd snatched the chance to marry again, then died. (Patsy's stepfather drank and, some said, abused her.) Because of this, the story went, Patsy accentuated the positive, and valued family life.

"I'd think that would have made her hate families, or men, or something," my mother argued with my grandmother, as if this explanation were somehow her fault.

If I was careful, I could sometimes catch my mother reverting back into the kind of bad daughter I was showing evidence of becoming myself; these glimpses were as exciting as spotting a rare bird.

"Not everyone thinks like you, Betty Lou," my grandmother said.

My mother had roughly what Patsy Long had, what she'd been sure she wanted—a workaday husband who did what was expected as faithfully as a cartoon. (Both my father and Patsy's husband forgot anniversaries until the last minute, then rushed out for Russell Stover candy; they could boil an egg if they were careful, but never scramble, poach, or fry. The workings of their own houses were mysteries to them, and they could not fathom the washing machines and ranges and air conditioners they financed.) Patsy thought this idiocy charming and treated her husband, Don, like the gigantic boy he was, taking off his black tie-up shoes when he propped them up at night in his lazy-boy recliner, listening to the dry trials and intrigues that occurred in his office, where he had somehow been elevated to comptroller of petroleum-based fertilizers.

"Oh, honey," she'd exclaim as he talked about his secretary's inefficiency or how he'd been cut off in mid-sentence by a member of the board. Thus she fueled his sulks, so that over the years his self-regard grew as large as his finicky appetite.

"Don only takes thighs. No salt for Don. He'll get a rash if you give him olives!"

She represented him at the table, half out of her seat, her cakelike breasts threatening the water glasses. Don's preferences were for gravy, milk, and pie, and everyone catered to his desire for the fat and bland. My mother, representative of the timely, the women's magazine, the pulse of the outside world, might bring over Oriental green beans or goulash supreme, but she and I—and occasionally my father—would be the only ones to try them.

"Looks good, Betty Lou, but we'll pass," Patsy Long would call out from behind her semicircle of gravy boats and milk jugs.

It had been difficult, but possible, to avoid Patsy Long when she'd been on her own. In her kitteny sweaters and soft, teased hair, she had been happy in her younger years to hum over the dish suds or curl up with Don as he snored and belched on the couch in front of the football games after dinner. But when she began to reproduce, my grandmother's house filled with her tiny offspring whenever we met for family dinners—no matter where you turned, there was someone pink and blond and smiling: Merry Ann, Terry Mae, Sherry Fae. Their names were enough to make you sick, my mother said.

I was always afraid my father might find Patsy Long appealing. It was not only Don who she'd cater and listen to—during a lull in her services she'd turn to any male around. She caused more than one fight in my family, the largest after she urged my father to rhapsodize about a girl he'd met in Italy during the war.

"I told you about her years ago," my father said to my mother on the way home.

"Oh, who cares," my mother muttered contradictorily; she had already slammed two doors.

I was sure that my mother saw what I had seen—that some hidden attractiveness of my father's blossomed before our very eyes when he was petted and pampered by Patsy Long. For us to regard my father as desirable, as sexy even, was not possible and would have required a monumental shift of perspective in our house.

As far as my mother was concerned, it was only briefly, during the tentative days of courtship, that such attention toward a man was warranted or worthwhile.

"Otherwise, you've just got another baby on your hands, who never grows up," she told me during one of her tirades against Patsy. I saw this myself, but in my secret heart I feared that at some point my mother would go too far in her scorn.

"You've got two legs, use them," she was always telling my father, before such pronouncements were in style. My father did use them—should have used them, I thought, but I worried about the threat of women like Patsy Long, who concerned themselves with the comfort of men. She was a pretty hen pecking around our perimeters and would have been surprised at how scared I was of her.

OVER the years, Patsy and my mother came to represent different sides of some philosophical argument I could never quite define. There were times when my mother came near to wishing her ill—when she could not hide, from me anyway, her private satisfaction in seeing Patsy's machinations backfire. Patsy had pumped up Don into believing he should be elevated to president of his company, an unfulfilled expectation that left him, most of his worklife, dissatisfied. With great reluctance, as her girls grew, Patsy was forced out of her kitcheny domain in order to finance the extracurricular activities she condoned. For a while she substitute taught home ec and typing, but it was hard for her to concentrate. She was always calling home to see that the girls were managing to grill their lunches without her, that Don took his ulcer medicine (a malady, my mother said, Patsy had caused). In fact, outside of her house, without an apron or the blush of cooking on her cheeks, Patsy Long seemed out of place and frowzy; eventually she was fired.

But in the scheme of things, these were minor discouragements, and there was painfully little for my mother to gloat about. To a large extent, Patsy was having what she said she wanted and the way she had said she wanted it.

PATSY LONG'S one child-rearing axiom was: Do what you want, but do it at home. No one actually believed she meant this, but it sounded good, and Patsy was an expert at things that sounded and tasted and felt good. She'd give you mini neckrubs whenever she passed you from behind—almost indecent they were in their fast intimacy—and pop things into your mouth when she passed from the front—peanut butter morsels and chocolate dobs—you never quite knew what they were and didn't want to spit them out to check.

My own mother had no such foolish rules or inclinations and was chock-full of lists of things she didn't want me doing anywhere: dating boys of certain races, hanging out on certain streets, along with a dizzying array of evidently pleasurable acts—smoking, drinking, necking. I think she knew I could not avoid them all, but hoped, by bargaining against so many, that I'd settle for a few. She was as mistaken in this as was Patsy Long, whose daughters called her bluff: there were so many boys in the Long house that it was impossible to keep track.

"Loretta, we've got someone for you to meet!" Patsy exclaimed as soon as we walked through her door, and there would be another one, undistinguishable from the one before him—big-armed, brown-haired, with sex in his eyes. If Patsy'd had her way, this unknown boy, not even of our family, would be allowed to take up the room and day. We'd hear about his nickname, his favorite foods, his prowess at sports. But my mother would somehow manage to deflect this by focusing—and exaggerating—some meager accomplishment of my own. I didn't mind being lied about as much as I hated hearing about myself at all. Unlike Merry and the others, who blushed and swelled when they were the center of attention, I became hot and morose. To hear in my mother the need to use me was almost unbearable.

"And then her music teacher said she had the most professional way of holding the clarinet of any student he's known."

But the worst was when my mother pinned me at the ravaged dining-room table and asked me, in effect, to represent myself.

"Loretta, tell them how your essay won the freshman prize."

These were among the most painful requests my mother would make of me in my life; I would be locked over my plate in a swarm of emotions—pity for her and her need to impress our petty extended family, hatred for the plump and pious Longs, whose blondness and brass had allowed them to believe they were somehow special. Besides, explaining how an essay had won was an impossibility. What was I supposed to do—chart the thought processes of a judge?

If I waited long enough to respond, Patsy made a transition from my silence. "Speaking of essays, Merry's Bob had one on animal husbandry, in the *Herald.*"

Across the valley of cold mashed potatoes, the picked chest of a turkey, my eye would be pulled back to what it was always pulled back to, the disappointment on my mother's face.

BECAUSE there was no one to compare me with before the Long girls were born, I was considered pretty. I never knew if it was a coincidence that this stopped after their arrival, or whether their astounding blondness merely deflected all other attention. People turned to them as they turned toward hot lights or loud noises on the television. They were bright more than they were any-thing—they even grew pale hair on their cheeks and arms, as soft as the newborn chicks we bought at Woolworth's for Easter. Besides their looks, the talents they possessed were the kind that were noticed. I won spelling bees and read the largest volume of books from the Bookmobile one summer, but the Longs starred in school plays, headed pageants, twirled tasseled batons.

Of course, this all occurred in my mother's hometown, Gil-bert, and as she said, "It's easy to be a big fish in a small town."

My mother had left Gilbert upon her marriage, and whenever she was with her family, grew proud of our town life in Union, twenty miles away. We had Gregg's, a two-floor department store, a civic auditorium, and a Chinese restaurant that specialized in pressed duck. Gilbert was just an old-people's town, she said. There was only Henk's Dress Shop downtown, where house-dresses began at size twenty, and the Time Out Café, where all meat was thrown in the deep fryer and everyone remembered what a fool you'd been when you were young. Gilbert was the only place where my mother was still known as Betty Lou, a name she thought so rural that she'd tossed it aside as soon as she moved to Union and called herself simply Bette.

My mother said it was a crime to raise daughters in a place of such limited possibilities. What did it mean to be chosen cheerleader when there were only six girls in town who could do cartwheels and half of them were out of school? And who wanted to spend a lifetime fighting ancient prejudices that in larger places, like Union, had been long ago diffused? In Gilbert, Catholics and Protestants still could not date or intermarry without considerable outrage from the parishes. And the only other outsiders were Mexican migrants who were trucked in to pick tomatoes in August, then trucked back out, under cover of darkness.

It was with a great and inexplicable spirit of diversity that my mother embraced Union, where people fought over other things— for example, there was a sizable population of blacks to spurn and dislike. But my mother, in the early, abstract time of our life there—when I was young enough to come home each twilight, as obedient as our beagle; when all I wished was to skirt the margins of our yard—was not worried about this. She even defended our town to Patsy Long, who was afraid to walk downtown in Union after dark.

"Your girls won't know how to act when they grow up if all they've had is Gilbert," my mother said.

IN those years, my mother still sewed for us both, following the newest patterns that could be found at Gregg's. She made us dirndl skirts and wool boleros and flannel capes that closely mimicked styles then in vogue out in the world. I liked to stand beside her in our matching box jackets with satin linings as we regarded the Longs, still in their hand-hemmed pastels. She made me feel that there in Union we were ambassadors of something big and new.

In fact, my mother was so impressed by fashion that my freshman year she made me the first miniskirt in all of Union, and she grew outraged when the dean of girls, Miss Hart, sent me home when I wore it to school the first day.

"How dare she!" my mother exploded when she read the note. I stood in front of the hallway mirror and considered myself as she went to the typewriter and began to write a response. Indecent, Miss Hanks had called this skirt, and I saw her point. It was so short that you could see the swell of my upper thighs, an area where I was already accumulating fat.

During the short hour I'd been in school, the principal, the janitor, boys I didn't even know, had all given me the most amazed and searing looks. Was it right for me to endure this just because it was the style in Milan?

According to my mother, who stood over her Smith Corona to read her note, the answer was yes.

Dear Miss Hart:
I suggest you refer to this month's *Women's Day* and the most recent Spiegel catalogue to acquaint yourself with current styles. In six weeks every girl in school will be wearing skirts like this, and there will be no way for you to stop it. I left my own hometown years ago to avoid such small-mindedness. Though my daughter is in the vanguard, I see no reason to punish her for it.

Sincerely, Bette Dardio.

My mother folded the note and sealed it in an envelope. "Okay, go and give this to Miss Hart."

"I don't want to wear this skirt anymore. Everybody stared at me."

"People always stare at new things."

"I mean boys."

"Oh, come on. Show a little spunk. I can't fight these battles for you."

But she was; she did, and I wasn't sure they were even battles worth fighting.

IN the following months the miniskirt trend bypassed Union like a tropical storm. The drama teacher wore one, once, to a cocktail lounge on the outskirts of town, but the mid-length pleats of the Long girls and others like them reigned, year in and out. Except in our house: my mother continued to sew these scraps of cloth in solids and prints—they were so tiny that she could whip one up in a day—and make me wear them.

Walking to school in the late autumn, trying to ignore the men in paneled trucks on North Street who jammed their brakes to eye me, I understood for the first time how the famous and handicapped must feel—to be noticed like this was a terrible thing. But I brazened it out all that fall until I got strep throat and it snowed, and my grandmother, on an impromptu visit with Patsy Long, dropped by and intervened on my behalf.

"I don't know what gets into you, Betty Lou," she yelled at my mother as she looked through my closet. "Allowing your own daughter to walk around half naked in this cold."

"Making me," I stressed.

"Oh, be a bunch of hicks, then," my mother exploded, slamming out of my room. "Wear an apron to school. I'll buy you saddle shoes! I'm not going to bother with any of you anymore."

IT turned out that my mother was wrong about so many things. The woman my father had an affair with later that winter was a blond named Conny Ann Baxter, who owned, of all things, a beauty salon. My father met her during his weekend job selling beauty supplies, a job my mother had insisted he take because he got underfoot in the house. *It would have been better not to know.* I heard my mother say this on the phone to someone, and I agreed with her on this, though little else.

Although I never wore a miniskirt again after that year, I had gained a certain reputation from the time that I had. Boys no longer jeered when they saw me, but scraped the toes of their shoes in the gravel to slow down their bikes. Some afternoons I sat expectantly for whole hours on our iced front stoop in my Glen plaid cape and gaucho pants. The world of girls I had always lived in split open, and underneath it lurked a place of illusion and artifice.

ALTHOUGH my father was returned to us by spring, sheepish, thinner, my mother had already retreated, perhaps into herself, although no one asked. Some nights there was only fried bologna for supper, unless I took it upon myself to open a can. I even began ordering my own clothes from Montgomery Ward's, only asking her for the check. And we managed to avoid the town of Gilbert altogether until that night when the local man orbited earth.

"A new era," Patsy Long whispered as she made tea towels from a pile of the lighter weight miniskirts that my grandmother had managed to confiscate. My mother mustered up enough of herself to disagree, but perhaps this was only habit. In spite of all her style, it seemed to me that she was still stuck at my grandmother's drop-leaf table, in Gilbert.

Life Insurance

IN his youth, my father presided as the King of the Rainbow Ball at the polytechnic school he attended, along with a young woman, who, unlike my mother, looked like Veronica Lake, her hair so cool and blond and sculpted that it seemed as if it were one gilded piece. This was the extent of my father's interesting accomplishments, as far as I was concerned when I was a girl. Other facts I duly noted, but they held little glamour for me. For example he left home on a warship when he was barely eighteen, and returned from this only trip he'd take to Europe with head lice and a German Luger, the latter of which he kept for years in his underwear drawer. After the war and the polytechnic and his brief stint as king, he met my mother at a local dance, where he claimed to have felt the tug of destiny, like some tidal pull, as they swayed in each other's arms. Following their wedding, he became an insurance agent, bought a vinyl briefcase, and developed heart disease.

My father's family's facts were only slightly more compelling. My grandfather's name was August, which made me wonder why some months were fine for names, but others were not. A sister was lost to diphtheria, a disease I thought must have disappeared because it was so difficult to spell. The family was so poor that they received only peppermints for Christmas; on a good year, walnuts.

This was an oral legacy that could not, of course,

cover everything. For example, I inherited a certain German ruddiness from my father, along with a short torso and his large— often aching, later ailing—heart. Watching him stammer in arguments, I also feared that I'd inherited his inarticulateness.

There was little time for my father and me as I was growing up; he managed chiefly to pick me up in his lap after dinner or occasionally sing me a song. His voice was so bad that it caused me substantial embarrassment when he sang in public. But there at home, when we were both full of food and my mother had briefly freed us from her critical eye, it would be as near a delight as any I knew for my father to sing "Oh Suzannah" or "Red River Valley," even though he often forgot the lyrics. Many of these songs were melancholy ("There is an old shanty in old shanty town. / The roof is so slanty, it touches the ground") and reflected what I viewed as my father's sad former life. Sometimes, between stanzas, a memory would rise up in his normally businesslike mind, and he would recollect it in a wondering voice, as if he couldn't believe it had lived there all along. But then my mother would enter the room to turn on the television or change the subject or, jarringly, open the blinds, and anything tender or reminiscent or intangible was instantly gone. It would be over, and as I grew older, it was over even without her intervention; little by little these interludes disappeared. So did my father, who spent progressively large parts of his life entering the living rooms of the newly married or the soon to be deceased, selling life insurance from his vinyl case in order to buy the potatoes my mother mashed for me, the succession of ballet shoes, clarinets, and piano lessons that I moved through, talentless, unable to excel at one. I was amazed that my father sold anything, for I believed this required charm. That he might display traits like this elsewhere wasn't clear to me until later on.

Later on I had grown from a good girl to a bad one, from an obedient platinum child who saved the lives of ants to a dish-water-blond teenager with candied lipstick spread over lips specializing in lies.

By this time my family barely touched. We'd never had a pet, because my mother worried in advance over household hair, but when I observed the arching necks of neighborhood dogs as they were being petted, I knew that this was what I was searching for also. Underneath the romance and guile I saw in movies, the grand posturings of love, I suspected this old yearning for touch lay at the root of it. But there was little tradition of this in any branch of my family—only the oldest and heftiest female relatives ever really let you hug them, allowed you to splay their breasts with your head, press into their flanks, which were still guarded against grease and desire by vast floral aprons. How love was consummated by ordinary humans, as opposed to movie stars, was left for years to my rather wild imagination. Did they rub feet or noses, like Eskimos? Did they stick out their tongues and lick, like cats? The arching and climbing I had witnessed in squirrels and dogs took a long, reluctant time to impress itself upon me. Hands and feet and noses I could imagine; the other I vainly hoped belonged to other species.

But the more I came to recognize my need for touch, the less likely it was that I would find it within my family. My father seemed especially careful never to have any physical contact with me: standing close in an elevator, I could feel him shift his girth imperceptibly away; on the rare occasion of an embrace, I felt him hold back. The body—it was a feared thing in my family, tended to only in the strictest of privacy. My mother covered her small breasts, as if wounded, the few times I barged in on her when she wasn't wearing a bra; the first and only time I glimpsed my father naked, he slammed the bathroom door. Gradually, fretfully, I put it all together. But even knowing, I moved toward the world of love with murky vision, hoping for better. As an impatient teenager with poor eyesight, this perhaps was unsurprising. Without glasses, which in my vanity I frequently left behind, I could only make out the vague range of a face, the density that meant a human body. Blind to detail, I advanced; to see too well, I already knew, would hurt me.

ON that night, as on many others, my family sat in the dining room finishing our evening meal. I appeared to be there, chewing beef, watching my brother suck out marrow, but I was already miles away. In the background there was bad news on the television: someone had died, far away. I didn't know why this was being broadcast, since people died nearby, daily. As we ate, my mother watched my father with the assortment of looks she often wore now, worry and bitterness and other things I could not decipher without my glasses. What I saw of my father's face looked cool and pink and collected. If his mood was to be ruined by hearing about my D in geometry or the black boy who my mother overheard me talking to on the extension, it would be later, when his stomach was full of beef and beer and his feet elevated in his lazy-boy recliner. Let her tell him, I thought bitterly; after all, nothing could be done about it. Certainly geometry, for example, was an open-and-closed topic. If I didn't study, it was because isosceles triangles did not spark my imagination. And my geometry teacher, Mrs. "Conkhead" Conkley, her hips so wide that she knocked desks astray as she moved menacingly down the aisles, surely could not force me to care. *You can't force me*; this was an update of an old refrain—*you can't make me*— that I used to jeer as a child. But the things I wouldn't do then— eat peas or dry off between my buttocks after a bath—seemed laughingly inconsequential now. This was serious stuff, my mother informed me—flunking school, telling lies, talking to black boys on the phone.

Dreamily I took my plate and went to the kitchen, not asking to be excused, a request I thought archaic now, and scraped my untouched food into the wastebasket. I was thinking of another kitchen where I had recently stood, being kissed in a corner. The owner of that kitchen was a black woman who was the cousin of my secret boyfriend, Wendell.

"Where do you think you're going?" My mother interrupted my thoughts as I dawdled at the kitchen mirror.

"There's a dance at the Y," I said, lowering my eyes to the sink full of dishes I would not help wash.

Standing behind me, my mother spoke to my reflection. "We'll see what your father says about that when he hears about your report card and the phone call. . . ."

She stopped, as if remembering that my father was a man who rarely had a word to say about anything, and handed me my glasses, which I'd left behind, as usual, not being able to see well enough to know where.

"Wear these," she said tiredly, "You're going to get eyestrain."

I negotiated a move away from her, glasses in hand. "It's only the YWCA, for God's sake. They even advertise that they're Christian. What more do you want?"

I was aware that this remark, in response to nothing, made little sense, but lately I could not control the spew of arguments that seemed to have lain for years dormant in my mouth. I headed for my bedroom steps just as the phone rang, but my mother, dawdling in the kitchen, picked it up before I had time. I stood listening to the silence, then her angry snort as she slammed the receiver down. It was Wendell, and he had hung up, but even this act was a form of communication, meaning that he would be meeting me at the dance later tonight. A shaft of triumph rose through me as I climbed the steps and put on my glasses.

They stayed on all the while I was preparing myself for the dance, since it was necessary for me to be acutely aware of any possible flaw in my appearance. Since there were so many—most of them unalterable, including the width of my hips, the size of my breasts, the length of my hair—it took me several hours to work with the few assets I had.

There was no doubt that this was going to be a big night; I could feel possibility pumping through my veins. Wendell had already hugged and rubbed and kissed me, and tonight I knew he was going to do more—something unnamed and totally original that only he and I could perform. I changed from slacks to skirts, rolled up waistbands, rolled them down, stuffed my bra. By the time I was ready and took off my glasses again, I had a headache from the mixture of hairspray and eau de cologne that hung around me like a cloud. I decided that I wouldn't dance much at the Y; I'd simply stand on the sidelines and wait for Wendell, so I wouldn't muss myself up.

I'd timed my departure so that I descended the stairs just as my mother was entering the shower. I had not reckoned on running into my father in the dark hallway, where I had paused to take another vague survey of myself in the mirror. I couldn't tell the look on his face—he often wore no look at all—but I knew that he wasn't smiling. I stood still, hoping he would pass, but instead, to my surprise, he flipped on the hallway light. Then he simply stared at me, standing there in that shocking brightness— a long, dismayed look that I felt more than saw. Had she told him about my report card, the phone call? I wondered as I banged out the back door, but the balminess of the spring night seduced my thoughts almost immediately away. Who cares, I said to myself, teetering down the driveway in my high heels. *Who the hell cares?*

WENDELL didn't show up at the YWCA dance that night, although it seemed as if every other black boy in town who even remotely resembled him did. I spent a number of feverish hours standing with a suitably blank face near the doorway, trying to decipher features, sense expectation, but it was no, not him,

time and time again. To top it all off, no one else even asked me
to dance. In order to distract myself from this, I talked halfheart-
edly to a few girls from my class, but their chatter seemed stupid.
What do they know about anything, I thought hatefully as they
exclaimed over boys—all white—who they did or did not like.
It occurred to me several times—disloyally to Wendell—that
perhaps I was being ignored by the other boys because I had
somehow miscalculated my appearance at home. Against my better
judgment, I checked out this theory in the fluorescent-lit bathroom, which was squealing with girls and busy with such a flurry
of combs and tubes that I sat on the toilet in the last stall until
everyone cleared out. Then I opened the door quickly, put on
my glasses, and took a fast, horrified look in the mirror. I was
wrong, all wrong, every centimeter. Too much makeup, too much
teasing—I blanched, remembering the baffled face of my father.

When I came back out, an eon of suffering later, the dance
had already begun to break up, and I walked out the door to a
side street. Away from the streetlights and roaring cars of my
peers, I put on my glasses, wiped away most of my makeup with
a Kleenex, and began to walk barefoot after kicking the high
heels from my aching feet. It was a long walk, but I didn't notice;
I was busy savoring the distinctive pain of Wendell's rejection. I
was near home, at the corner of High Street, when I felt a car
advancing behind me; before I could rip off my glasses or prepare
myself in any way, Wendell's face was idling beside me in the
passenger side of someone else's car. When he opened the door,
I was revealed in all my disheveledness by the inner light. Wendell looked at me in disbelief, and I saw whatever regard might
have once been there evaporate, right on the corner of Rosewood and High. Finally he got out of the car.

"Somebody said they'd seen you walking off, and I wanted to
catch you."

I stood there, surely caught, but unsure what to say.

"See, I was heading into the dance," he continued. "But your father stopped me in the parking lot and said he wanted to talk."

"My father!"

"Yeah." Wendell chuckled and handed me a slip of white paper. "He even gave me his card." He scratched his head, avoiding my eye. "He said he didn't want us to see each other no more. I didn't know you were gonna tell him."

"I *didn't* tell him!" I exploded.

"Listen, Loretta, I don't need to be getting into any mess with nobody's people. I dig you and all . . ."

"What else did he say?"

"I told you," Wendell said, moving away enough to place his dark hand on the chrome of the door handle. When I heard the button click, I moved off a bit myself, not wanting to be illuminated again.

"So I guess we'd better cool it awhile," he said as he got in, but I was already heading barefoot down Rosewood.

A few minutes later, as I walked up our driveway, my father's car purred in behind me. Standing in the heat of his headlights, I looked down for the first time at the card I'd been clutching in my hand:

> WILLIAM "BUD" DARDIO
> INDEPENDENT AGENT
> LIFE INSURANCE
> 229 EAST ROSEWOOD

Even after the lights went out, I touched the vellum, the raised type that felt like Braille. Of all the finales I'd planned for this evening, how could I have ever thought up this? But there I was, barefoot on asphalt, thwarted by my father and his card.

Gregg's

GREGG'S— not a boy's possessive, as I thought as a girl; not a family name even, I later discovered. Just the name, surely signifying something or someone, of the department store that was once the center of our small Ohio town—all there was of it, really. Because of this, it contained everything: islands of candy and cologne, departments for bowling balls, and bridal gowns, a beauty salon called the Clip Joint, even a greasy restaurant on the second floor.

Salesclerks at Gregg's had worked there so long that they had become identified by what they sold. There was the lingerie woman, who went to our church; she swished when she walked, presumably from the satin slips she bought there on discount. There was the hosiery woman, dark and divorced, who was forever extending her arm through stockings to demonstrate shade; the Estée Lauder clerk, elaborately curled and reeking of Youth Dew. These women had worked at Gregg's all their lives and would work nowhere else; if you walked in first thing in the morning, they would be stationed proprietarily behind their counters, as if at their own front doors.

Growing up in our town was done in conjunction with Gregg's, where lives were chronicled by the salesclerks, who presided over you even *in utero*. Mothers bought maternity dresses there, and that's how much of the town discovered they were pregnant. Bassinets were bought, then baby clothes—this stretched all the way through saddle shoes and sanitary belts, and then, with engagement rings, the cycle began all over again.

It was not a women's store, but it was mostly women who were there. The black elevator operator, wearing one silver glove, took eternal trips to the second floor, announcing in a languid voice after each chimed arrival, "Lingerie, housewares, maternity, coffee shop" as she pulled open her grate to let the whites pass by. She wouldn't let you catch her eye, and said "Watch your step" with great generality, certainly not meaning *you*. The corner of her elevator was furnished with a stool, her other glove, and a magazine called *Jet*, but I never saw her sit, put on the other glove, or read anything during the years she transported us up and down. And because she didn't wear a nametag like the other salesladies, who had decided to be known as Mrs. James Polk or Mrs. Ricki Klinger, in conjunction with the husbands they had acquired long ago, she remained nameless to me.

Not so Clara, the old woman in Gregg's bathroom, who was there every time I went in throughout the years, first for genuine physical reasons, too low and egoless to even notice the well-lit mirrors, later to smear on forbidden eye shadow and smoke even more forbidden cigarettes.

Clara would be stationed on the vinyl sofa in the lounge, surrounded by Gregg's bags, which seemed to validate her presence, as if she were always just finishing up some interminable, exhausting spree. But unlike the elevator woman, who was silent except when professional necessity required her to speak, Clara talked chronically, in complaints that ushered forth from a mouth dark as a bruise, but filled in at the center, like a tart, with a sour orange color.

"Did you notice the ice in front of the store?" she would ask you or anyone, and no matter how you responded, or even if you didn't respond at all, she would forge on. "Well, I almost broke my neck coming in, and it wasn't the first time. I told Helene down in jewelry that they're going to end up in court unless someone takes steps."

Often enough there was another old lady around who, with legitimately tired feet and a new bag of goods, was perfectly willing to grouse with Clara for a few minutes while she caught her breath. I liked to watch the way women who were strangers became intimately connected through complaint. It was clear Clara liked it also; her old cheeks bloomed when someone else was incited to indignation by her efforts. But other women, especially other younger women like my mother, did not pay her much mind, and wore the mostly deaf, partly amused expression that I knew was used by people who thought themselves superior.

Once when my mother found me sitting with Clara, listening intently to her account of how she was being repeatedly gypped at the candy counter, she grasped my wrist and sharply maneuvered me away.

"What are you doing? She's crazy," she hissed once we were outside.

"She is not," I said hotly. "She's just an old woman . . ."

"Who lives in the bathroom of a department store. Don't you think that's a little strange? I hear they've been trying to get rid of her for ages."

"She's got a right—" I began. I had recently become big on rights and everyone having them, but my mother interrupted again.

"Just be quiet. I've got a headache, and we still haven't gotten what we came for."

What we had come for was a blouse to complete my uniform for the marching band, which my mother did not yet know I had no intention of joining. This was one of the many wrong assumptions she had begun making around this time—that just because I'd been first-chair clarinet in the orchestra throughout my early years, I would automatically agree to march around a football field now that I was in junior high.

Since she hadn't asked me how I felt about this, I decided that there was no reason to feel guilty as she rummaged through racks of blouses, searching for a large girl's size. One of the clerks, who we knew well by then because we'd clothed my budding body from her territory for years, finally approached us and helped my mother look.

"You know, she's practically as big as you are," she told my mother after they had searched in vain. "Why don't you go over to Ladies."

My mother stopped and studied me, then without a word led the way out of the girls' department, that side of the first floor cordoned off for the petite, the innocent, the not-yet-formed, and we never entered it again.

As we headed for Ladies, my mother remembered a blouse she had just received—one of my father's many ill-chosen gifts—that would surely fit me. She said it would save her from having to return it; she didn't say that it would also keep her from dwelling on the fact that after fifteen years of marriage my father still did not have the dimmest notion of what she would or wouldn't wear. Because of this, for the first time in my memory we left Gregg's empty-handed, without the small thrill of carrying a glossy red stapled bag containing an item that back home would become utterly ordinary.

The fact that it was my mother's blouse, presented earlier by my muddled father, made the treachery of my deceit, when it was discovered, somehow more severe. I set off for school docilely enough the next morning, wearing that blouse, but with no intention of going to the first band practice, scheduled for last period. I had never skipped a class before, but saw I would have no compunction about doing so now. Playing in an orchestra had been one thing; marching in front of people in baggy wool pants and a plumed helmet was another. My mother had been in a marching band in her youth and considered it her heyday, but that wasn't my problem. Without a pang I spent sixth period in a bathroom stall with my clarinet case, reading *Glamour* Do's and Don'ts.

MY mother found me out, of course; later on, I saw that she would always find me out, but never be able to prevent my lying, which she was sure started on this date.

"How was practice?" she asked—a bit too brightly, I thought—first thing when I walked in that afternoon.

"OK."

I took off my jacket, but kept my clarinet in hand, as if to look more authentic.

"Meet any new kids?"

"No, just the usual."

"Like who?"

"Oh, Vicki Harter and them." By now I was feeling suspicious, and I never really forgave my mother for pushing me like that, for making me lie more than I had to.

"Well, that's very interesting, since I just got a call from Mr. Rosner asking why you didn't come."

"Oh," I said, hating already the feeling that spread through me and that in the future would be common.

"So?" she prompted.

"So, nothing. I didn't want to go, that's all. I don't want to go. I'm not."

"You're not." She smiled falsely, tapping her foot like a wife on the "Honeymooners."

Those words—"I'm not"—felt good to me, solid and powerful, and I could tell that my mother knew she was in trouble.

"Don't you think you could've discussed this with me and spared

me the embarrassment of having that man call like you're some
. . . truant?"

"You never discuss anything," I mumbled, turning to leave the
room and my clarinet—I was sick of it suddenly, always waiting passively for me to blow it, and of this room, so full of my
mother.

"Just a moment there, miss."

"No, you never listen, that's what you never do," I hesitated
to say, and then I really did leave the room.

I was punished for this, naturally, but even my mother knew
it hadn't much weight or sting. The first punishment was being
grounded for a week, which meant missing a pep rally that I
didn't want to go to anyhow. The second, smaller punishment
was having to return my mother's blouse to Gregg's, even though
it had been worn.

"I don't care about that. Take it back. I don't want it around
the house," she cried. "And I'd like the receipt, thank you very
much, and every nickel of change."

BY the time I reached Gregg's by bus, it was almost dusk and
the store was nearly empty, since most women were off fixing
dinner somewhere. It was an odd hour, one that I found both
exciting and melancholy, suggesting places I might just be, but
was not. Even the salesladies seemed discombobulated, as if they
knew, deep down, that they should really be home.

I was not used to the salesclerks in Ladies, and no one seemed
to recognize me. I disturbed their dinner break, which got me off
on the wrong foot straightaway, but I already felt the transaction
was doomed.

"This has been worn!" the clerk said as she pulled the blouse
from the bag, and then, to my surprise, she sniffed the armpits.
"It even smells!"

"I told my mother that," I began, like the coward I was, but this only made it worse.

"Well, you can inform your mother that Gregg's does not take back worn, stained, or smelly merchandise," the clerk said smartly, and stuffed the blouse in the bag before flouncing back to her group, who gave me a collective look of scorn.

Even after such a rebuke, I found that I didn't want to return home just yet, to the predictable scene awaiting me there. I dawdled by the roasted nuts, my favorite department, but I had only enough money for one eighth pound of split cashews—hardly a treat. Still, just that they were there, hot and fragrant, was pleasant, even if they weren't for me, and I felt all at once the comfort of that old, grand store, even with its evil salesclerks—even so.

I ended up in the bathroom for no real reason; at that point I had not yet taken up smoking and was not in the mood for eye makeup. There was no place I wanted to go tonight, no one I wanted to see. Or so I thought, until I noticed Clara, who was rummaging through her bags, in which I could see for the first time hair rollers, sliced bread, rain hats, napkins, apples—a whole jumbled female life. Seeing her there, planted so firmly with so little, comforted me. It was an apple that she was fishing for, but she quickly dropped it back in her bag when I sat down.

"Well, I guess this is it," she said after a moment in her usual tone.

"What?"

"Winter. I told them downstairs that the store isn't heated like it should be. Don't you think it's cold in here?"

I wanted to keep her talking, but was out of the lying mode and shook my head no.

"I do," she said, but without much punch. It was nearly six o'clock, after all; surely she had been at it all day.

We sat in silence awhile, but I didn't care; my mind was busy. Where did this old woman go at night with her bags and chatter?

How could she be as alone as she seemed to be? I wanted to ask these things, but this did not seem the place for questions; both of us had retreated here, and that seemed to make it a sanctuary.

Eventually I felt her discomfort with our silence; I stole a glance and saw that her mouth looked puzzled, as if it didn't know what to do with itself unless it made noise.

"It is a little chilly," I finally conceded, and that seemed to be enough. In any event, she bent to retrieve her motley apple, which she rubbed and sliced and, eventually, shared with me.

I SAW Clara again during the four more years I lived in our town before leaving for college, but we were not alone like that again. Gregg's fell onto hard times soon after my departure, when malls sprang up on the outskirts of town. But I didn't realize how far things had gone until my visit home the week before my college graduation. My mother insisted on buying me a new coat as a present—she disapproved of the ratty one I always wore—and before I knew it, she was herding me into the car and we were headed for one of the malls.

"I hate those places," I told her. "Why don't we just go over to Gregg's?"

She laughed. "Gregg's closed ages ago. They're demolishing it this weekend to build some office complex."

"They're *not*," I said, and saw the satisfaction on my mother's face. It wasn't often now that she could shock me. "We could still drive by."

"The streets are probably closed, plus there's nothing left," she said.

So we drove to the mall, and I let my mother spend too much money on a coat that I didn't like and knew I'd rarely wear. She didn't ask me, I thought as I watched the money exchange hands.

But later that night after dinner I left the house, saying I was visiting a friend, and walked the dark sidewalks to Gregg's instead.

My mother was wrong on one hand—the streets weren't closed—but right on the other; there was nothing left. Still, I walked around, kicking bits of rubble until I found an old shopping bag, almost glossy, still red. Then I slung it over my arm and stood there in the ruins, thinking how cold Clara would have found this particular night.

Reunion

IT'S 1964, and this is my father's family reunion: my father's last living brother, Johnny, his family, my parents, and I, congregated at a picnic table under a tree dying of Dutch elm disease.

Johnny and his wife, Marion, are around the same age as my parents and have an only daughter, Louise. After unloading their coolers, Marion and my mother sit together in unhappy alliance, being, without liking it, roughly in the same boat. But their differences are glaringly apparent, especially to me.

Marion smokes filter-tipped Kents while talking about her job as an LPN at Valley Hospital, where, she frequently lets us know, she has seen just about everything. In her world-weary way, she drones on about victims of motorcycle accidents, about blacks who knife each other in the chest; Marion herself has removed switchblades a number of times. Cigarette after cigarette she smokes, filling the yard with a slightly perfumed scent.

Marion is usually flanked by her mother, Mrs. Willey, who lives in the basement of Johnny and Marion's house. She lived there with her husband until he died—a bullied, unhappy man, as thin as she is enormous—her housedresses straining at their mother-of-pearl buttons.

Any opinion from either Marion or her mother was sure to be controversial. They both disapproved of Catholics, especially the pope, and, more particularly, nuns. They couldn't fathom why any woman would marry Jesus, an ancient, possibly mythical man, although they defended him at other times, for their own reasons, as a kind of hapless hero who had their souls generally in mind. They were for law and order, but could not bear the Italian police officers and their bleached young wives who lived in duplexes on their block. Where were they when Marion's tire blew out in the middle of the night on Route 29, not a mile from a ghetto? Both mother and daughter were Republican, unless one was in power, and then they would be renegades and vote Democrat. Alternately they'd be neither, saying that both parties were corrupt, so why bother voting at all? For a time they idolized the surgeons Marion mixed with in the emergency room. She was forever parroting their opinions and diagnoses, until one of them slighted or ignored her or insinuated that she should remember her minimal role as a nurse. Then she turned against them all, calling them charla-tans who had probably been put through medical school by their wives.

It was in this strangely feminist vein that Marion often veered off—she was especially fierce about husbands taking advantage of their wives. Left and right, in their very neighborhood, no less than five men in their forties had packed their bags and simply taken off. She ticked them off on her yellowed fingers, noting their exceptional jobs: "One a civil engineer, one a dentist, another with a good job on the railroad, all giving their money to young women, when who do you think got them where they are today? Their wives!"

To avoid these conversations, I played with Louise, but I didn't much like her. She was squashed by her mother and grand-mother, a docile girl who had a faint mustache and thick glasses that smudged her brown eyes. She wore Scotch-plaid skirts that made her look as if she had an unusually frumpish, matronly behind, and, although nothing was wrong with her arches, orthopedic shoes. My mother, who flipped through plenty of

Spiegel catalogues, said it was a shame how Marion bullied her.

For it was when discussing Louise that Marion's voice reached the pinnacle of indignation—oh, she had such plans for her daughter's life! Louise and I could hear her thrilling voice from across the yard as we sorted boxes of buttons or sank desolately into a comic-book romance. Between the ages of eighteen and twenty, Louise was to marry a Methodist between 5′11″ and 6′1″. He should be of more than middle-class potential, a budding salesman or civil servant, and happy to support Louise's higher education.

Juxtaposed with Marion, my mother seemed a champion of personal freedom.

"She's going to push that girl out in the street with all her planning," my mother said. "And have you ever seen anklets on a girl her age?"

She addressed these comments to me during our rides home, since, as she often noted, my father was so oblivious to the nuances of style that we could have walked around the house in potato sacks. It was thrilling to be her confidante at times like these, although she did not know that my allegiance to her was circumstantial and fleeting.

"The kids at school would laugh her right out of the room," I said hotly, leaning over the front seat at her neck. "Do you know what subject she likes best at school? Math!"

My mother laughed, although I didn't even know what I meant—what was so wrong with liking math? But this was how close we were during those brief summers before I was separated from her forever by deceit and womanhood and sex. Using this to my advantage for the first and last time, I talked her into buying me contact lenses, saying that with glasses I thought I looked like Louise.

From year to year it was I, not Louise, who drastically changed, who grew out of fashions that altered before I'd had the chance to get them right. She remained slightly plump and mustachioed, in the same plaid skirts and homely vests. But different as we were, I needed someone to talk to that summer of 1964, and Louise was all there was. We no longer sorted buttons or gingerly tore out perforated cocktail dresses for our paper dolls, but sat like adults on aluminum chairs, grilling silently in the sun.

That summer I had a secret in my pocket—a yarn-wrapped ring from a boy my parents disapproved of named Greg Todd. Later in the afternoon, when I got Louise alone, I told her in tedious detail the story of our love: how the only reason my parents disapproved was because Greg went to South High on the other side of the tracks and because his cousin, also named Greg, once stole beer from a carry-out. I told her roughly how far we had gone—which I thought she would certainly want to know—that he had partially unbuttoned my blouse in a pickup truck in the parking lot after he had given me this ring; how we'd already had our first fight only a night ago because I had discouraged him from unbuttoning further as we stood in the alley between Trinity Methodist and Bill Dahl's Buick, a place, I told her, where all the kids went to neck. I told her that I had a pink princess phone in my bedroom and talked to Greg every night between eight and nine under cover of "McHale's Navy" or "The Honeymooners." I insisted that my parents did not—could not—know. I even gave Louise my ring to hold, and at one point in my story she put it on. It was a cheap ring and, compared to the heavy, multiple bands that my mother and Marion wore, must have looked like a display of the most fleeting, superficial affection.

When I had finished, I sat silent and waited for Louise's reaction, but she only handed back my ring and looked at me slightly, as if too much would either taint her or hurt her eyes. She said nothing but began to examine a mosquito bite on her thigh. I couldn't believe her lack of conspiracy. A few minutes later she said that she had to go to the bathroom. When she didn't return, I found her sitting between Marion and Mrs. Willey on the other side of the yard. My mother was serving them lemonade from a pitcher while Mrs. Willey was saying in a querulous voice, "A glass of water would quench your thirst faster than that."

A week later my mother received a letter from Marion, who typically wrote only when there was some family tragedy to transmit. Louise had told her my whole shameful story, and she just wanted to let my mother know, since "it's easy to lose control of girls this age." However, she stressed that she'd had no such trouble herself.

My mother didn't show me the letter, but I read it secretly one night when she was out. It was written on Valley Hospital stationery, so that my crimes looked more official.

That letter began the slow change of terms between my mother and me. Not only had I lied to her again, but now I had done it in a fashion that made her look a fool. It was this latter point that seemed to bother her most, and for years after she refused to go to my father's reunions, saying she had no intention of being scoffed at.

My parents began to go again, at my father's insistence, the year I turned sixteen, the same summer that Louise, exactly on cue, married a Methodist named Darrell Fink, who successfully sold office supplies and was delighted to finance Louise's business-school education—she was going to be a legal secretary, a career Marion thought highly of.

The newlyweds were at the reunion, and my mother told me in long detail about the wedding photos—Louise wore an ivory Sears gown, and Darrell rented a tux. She talked about the twenty-one-foot house trailer that they purchased to place in the back lot behind Marion and Johnny's house. Marion planned to baby-sit after they had their first child, who Louise would name either Tammy or Burdette. My mother told me all these plans with a distinct lack of zest, since she was phoning me at a home for unwed mothers in another town, where I was spending five months, hot and sad and pregnant.

"I told everyone that we sent you to a private school now that the public ones are so bad. Louise said she was sorry you couldn't make it to her wedding. She wanted to show you her ring."

I snorted at that, but my mother didn't respond. In fact, she fell silent for so long that I thought something was wrong with our line.

"Mom—"

"I thought it was pretty," she said.

Wearing Green

AT that time, when my family went to Silver Lake for vacations, my brother and I were still comrades, sequestered in the backseat, away from my parents and their cigarette smoke and the lilting big-band music on the radio. I was proud of these vacations on a number of counts: Silver Lake was across state lines in Kokomo, Indiana, and a hundred miles away. This was something I bragged about to our baby-sitter, Caroline Rogers—a round, jovial girl who seemed to marry the moment we outgrew her assistance. I was thrilled by that number: I thought a hundred dollars a fortune, a hundred years an unthinkable length of time. But a few years later, when my brother told a schoolmate of mine that I weighed a hundred pounds, the number had lost its thrill forever, and the two of us had grown irrevocably apart.

I was also proud about Silver Lake because the rest of my family either did not take vacations or merged them with other necessary tasks. My grandmother and grandfather went to Cleveland for an extended weekend every year when it was time for my grandmother's hearing aid to be serviced; my aunt and uncle sometimes ventured as far as Dayton or Chillicothe but only in conjunction with the Jaycees or Band Camp.

Neither of my parents had taken vacations in their youth, although my father had gone off to Europe for the war. It was a trip that he sometimes spoke of with a certain longing, though I remembered other stories of his well enough to know that it must have been an altogether gruesome journey. He sometimes talked about the Viso Mountains, where he had once driven a jeep at night without any headlights, simply by the feel of the road. This jeep story was a favorite of his and had been told so many times, in situations where he had to quickly and decisively prove his worth, that it was now a joke, and my mother rolled her eyes each time he started it, and supplied the last line in a jeering voice, "Yes, we know, *by the feel of the road.*" When I was young, this account gave me a certain feeling of safety, which other stories over the years managed to revoke. Once, while courting my mother, my father fell asleep at the wheel and drove his Chevy into a tree on a winding country road. He was found the next morning by a farmer and was unconscious for several days. I thought my parents should not have told me this story if they expected me to sit trusting in the back of our car. As in many cases when I was growing up, I thought them imprudent, rash. They seemed often to go too far.

At Silver Lake, we stayed in an efficiency cabin with a screened-in porch, and my mother spent the first day spraying Lysol around the toilet and the tiles of the shower and changing the gray sheets with fresh percale ones she brought from home. While she swept and sprayed and dusted, my father walked down the sandy path to the lake and jumped into the water, his large, black-haired body floating first, then swimming past the ropes with strong, sure arms. He did not pay much attention to my brother and me, and seemed to enter the water with a commitment, a compulsion to enjoy himself. At that time he was still selling life insurance and had been told by his doctor that he was under too much stress, that he had to learn to relax. These vacations, then, were designed and executed by my mother, who began to wear a certain hooded, worried look when she watched my father—the same way she looked at her dinner when there were unexpected guests—as if she were afraid he wouldn't last.

It would be going too far to say that my mother actually enjoyed these vacations. She was simply there, as she was at home, or at church, or visiting my grandmother. She was bothered—no, irritated—by so many things: the mosquitoes, the sand on our feet, the heat in the cabin were all items that deeply vexed her. If it was raining any morning when we woke up, she would be personally chagrined. "Of course," she would say, looking out the window, "I knew it wouldn't last." She was annoyed by the way my brother and I haggled in the hot backseat about who would lie down and who would sit, and the way we watched each other's plates in restaurants with a desperate vigilance, to make certain we weren't being shortchanged. She was exasperated by our lack of interest in sightseeing—she was the only one who wanted to go into the town of Kokomo to see the war memorial or the new shopping mall or the Early American Museum with its roped-in rooms of spinning wheels and velvet furniture. This did not mean we did not go, but that we did not want to, and managed to ruin her trip by our own lack of zest. My father did not like these side trips either, but also went doggedly along. I sometimes heard them fighting through the thin beaverboard of the cabin walls as my mother rushed us to dress.

"I thought this was supposed to be a vacation, and all you want to do is hurry up and go."

"I can't sit in this cabin all night with those kids. There isn't even a TV."

"Well, we'll get a TV then. You're the one who didn't want to pay extra."

"Oh, it's me of course. It's always me."

It was always my mother; who could help but see her as the culprit? If it had been only my father, we would have probably stayed at the lake all day and even into the night, coming home with sand in our hair and buckets of rainbow fish that my mother always made us throw back because she didn't want to clean them.

"I'm not spending my time cooking you all supper. I can do that at home," she said. But wasn't she the one who insisted on making us homemade sandwiches of slick bologna instead of letting us go to the tempting snack bar at the beach? My mother did not make sense; she wasn't supposed to, we decided.

So, most evenings during our vacation, my brother and I would stand desolately under statues of men on rearing horses; in the doorways of antique shops that had menacing, handwritten signs exclaiming, "If you break, you buy!"; or in quaint turn-of-the-century restaurants where we wanted nothing on the menus. We only fought then out of boredom, because there was nothing left for us to do but enjoy what our mother had planned for us, and we did not intend to go that far.

My brother was still young enough then for me to consider him my appendage. Back home, I dressed him up in tulle and velvet and sent him out for the neighbors to laugh at; I told him large, elaborate lies that I never bothered to correct, so that for years he thought you pronounced the s in island, that honey was the urine of bees. My mother tried to monitor my behavior, but she was not around enough, or vigilant enough, to do any good. She said that I was cruel, that I should have more "natural" feelings for him, but I thought I had, and did not know what she meant.

I did not know many things, or did not understand them, especially that year I turned thirteen, the last year, in fact, that we went to Silver Lake for vacation. As reward for his insurance sales, my father was to win a series of trips in the following years to more exotic places—Hollywood, Florida, and St. Louis—trips that my brother and I would not be included on. I did not care because I suddenly saw our vacations in all their shabbiness. The cabin was too small, the lake too murky; a hundred miles took only an hour and a half to drive, and I'd heard that planes went that far in half an hour.

In that one summer, something major had changed in me, and I couldn't name what it was. But I had taken to kissing my father full on the lips when he was asleep in his armchair. I would plan this act for whole minutes and wait until no one else was in the room. I had also kissed Jimmy Michaels, a boy who lived across the street in a low, beer-smelling house. And I had actually lain in bed one afternoon with my next door neighbor, Carol, who suggested that we pretend to be husband and wife. I told my mother about each of these incidents in a paroxysm of guilt, but she didn't say anything, only looked dismayed, as if she wished I hadn't bothered. And that year, just before we left on vacation, there had been several terrible discoveries. One involved an explanation of intercourse that my mother read to me from *Growing Up and Liking It*, a pamphlet she received from the Kotex Company.

"You do that to each other?" I asked in anguish, and she nodded her head, solemnly. Yes.

Then she took out a pamphlet that had the profile of a woman's body with black arrows pointing to certain parts.

"You're going to be wearing a bra soon," she told me as I looked at it. "But don't ever say breasts, especially to boys. Call them bumps."

"Bumps?"

"But don't even say that. There's no reason for you to talk about them."

And the next month there was my period and another anxious talk, this time in the bathroom, where my mother gave me a Tampax, a diagram, then shut me in, and herself out.

"This doesn't fit," I called through the door. "There's no place for it to go."

"Yes, there is. Keep trying. You've got to relax."

So that last summer, as we pulled away from Silver Lake, I saw a distinctly altered reflection staring back at me in the rearview mirror. Watching my brother hour after hour in the shadowy backseat, I eventually turned him into Rick Hoffman, a boy in school who I had a hopeless crush on. While my mother slept, I leaned over and began kissing his face. He responded, and for a few moments we kissed furiously until she turned around at the sudden silence and pulled me up by my hair.

"That's incest! For God's sake, do I have to watch you every minute?"

She made my father stop the car, and climbed into the backseat between the two of us. My brother, dazed and sweaty, immediately went to sleep.

My brother does not remember this incident, or claims not to, for reasons, probably sound ones, of his own. He also does not remember another one that occurred a few years later.

It was a Saturday night when my parents were out for one of their rare Mutual of Omaha dinners, and I had decided to sneak my current boyfriend, a black boy named Tony Laws, up into my bedroom. It was eight o'clock, and my brother showed no signs of tiring; in fact, he was watching an episode of "Bonanza" with annoying zest.

"Why don't you come down into the basement, and I'll teach you to play the piano," I said to him. A year from then he would have said, "I'm watching TV," or "Why do you want to teach me piano all of a sudden?" or, even more likely, "What do you want?" But this was the last year I still had some control over him, and I felt a small twinge of shame at his surprised, trusting eyes. He trailed after me down to the basement, where our piano sat like a giant relic, painted by my mother over the years in her various styles of furniture refinishing: green, blue, and now a rococo antique white.

I had only recently discontinued my own piano lessons, a five-year fiasco with a teacher named Miss Birch, who led me through the John Thompson series and several Methodist hymnals before declaring to my family that I had neither talent nor sufficient discipline. But the disintegrating sheet music on the piano were antiques from my grandmother—"Yes, We Have No Bananas" and "Barney Google with the Goo Goo Googley Eyes!" I picked "Bananas" because I knew it well; in fact, my mother used to sing it in her younger, lighter days, as a lark. I had forgotten to calculate that my brother had never been near a keyboard, and it took me nearly half an hour to lead him through the scale. As he began playing a simple exercise, I heard a small knock at our back door.

"Stay here," I said. "I'll be right back." I ran up into our guest bathroom, where I used a swipe of my mother's coral lipstick, which she had shaped in her fashion, to a point. I caught my reflection in the mirror and was dismayed that I didn't look right; it would have taken a long while to cover up a small crop of pimples that had sprung up on my chin, and to straighten my bangs, which were lifted on the end into damp, lifeless curls. I even considered this, leaving Tony standing outside in the alien darkness, but it was too dangerous, especially when I opened the door and saw what he wore—a bright green iridescent slack-and-shirt set.

"We have to be quiet," I told him when I opened the door and took him by the hand, thinking that he would have assumed this, calculated the prejudices of my family, who he had never seen before, of our neighborhood, where he'd never been.

"Why?" Tony asked when we got to the steps. Then he heard my brother's desultory playing below us—"Yes, we have no bananas today. We've got . . ." —and a certain combination of anger and exasperation crossed his dark face. What did we know of each other, after all? Through some amateurish seduction on my part, we had ended up here at this most intimate spot—the bottom of my bedroom steps.

"I'm going," he started. "I'm not sneaking around nobody's house."

"No, don't," I whispered, leading him up the steps. "Just come up here, and it will be all right. Really. Come on."

When we reached my attic bedroom, he pulled me to his chest, but I said, "Let me get rid of my brother," and knew as I hurried back down that there would have to be retribution on my part for his humiliation, that I most certainly would have to do whatever he wanted.

My brother had his head in the refrigerator when I entered the kitchen.

"Why aren't you practicing?" I shouted.

"I don't want to anymore."

He was pouring himself a glass of flat Seven-Up and eating brownies out of the cake pan with his fingers, something he would have never been allowed had my mother been home. I sat down at the table and watched him, biting my nails; I don't think I had ever observed him so closely. Here in this small body was the same mix of genes that existed in me—how they had collided and split and merged to create such an opposite human was a mystery.

"It's getting late," I said, looking at the clock. "I think we should go to bed."

"Why? They aren't coming back till midnight; Caroline let us stay up till eleven."

"Well, I'm not Caroline," I snapped. "And I'll tell Mom you were eating brownies and wouldn't mind."

My brother looked up slowly; he was not stupid, and knew this was a pitiful, uncompelling argument—my mother would have paid little attention to my accusations. But he stood up, put the brownies back in the refrigerator, and headed toward his room. I stayed in the kitchen, turning off the lights and studying myself, as I did endlessly, in the square of mirror over our sink, where my mother had hung curtains so it looked like a window. I heard my brother's steps muted by the living-room carpet; then he hesitated by my bedroom steps where he made a brief cry.

He ran back into the kitchen, his face scarlet.

"There's a man on the steps! I saw him!" he said. "He's wearing green and he's just standing there. Come on!"

He took my hand, as if he were going to lead me to safety, but I knew there was no place he actually intended to go.

"Oh, you're seeing things," I said. "It's late, and you're tired."

"I am not! I saw him. Come on—maybe we should call the police."

"Calm down," I said, wiping my hands on a towel, and followed him to the steps, where Tony had thankfully moved off.

"But he's still up there, I know it. I want to call the Davises' and talk to Mom."

"We can't worry them," I said. "You're just seeing things. Come on and go to bed."

The night was wearing on me. I suddenly saw the combination of things that could have, and had, gone wrong. It was wearing on my brother also; his fright seemed to have diminished him, and by the time he had changed into his cowboy pajamas, he looked pitiful to me, frighteningly small.

"Lay down with me, just a minute," he said. "I'm scared."

"Well, I'm not," I insisted. "Now, watch. I'll walk up the steps and search the room, and then call down."

If this seemed a strange arrangement to him, he didn't say so, but stood at the bottom of the steps as I walked up with false heroism, touching Tony's hand as I passed him slumped unhappily on my bed.

"Everything's OK, see?" I called down to my brother. "Now go on and get in bed."

He did, and went to sleep almost immediately; I could hear

his tiny snore, a miniature replica of my father's, in only a few minutes.

It occurs to me now that I may have lost more than I gained that night. Although my brother seemed to have forgotten the incident by morning, he never totally trusted me again. I forfeited the chance, possibly the only one I ever had, to comfort him, and went up to Tony Laws instead. For his part, Tony was so humiliated by my conduct and his role as a frightening criminal that we never saw each other after that, although I did my best for him that night—let him pull off my skirt and panty hose, let him touch me there and there. But I knew it wasn't enough to make him forget.

My best wasn't enough. This was a line from a song that I listened to later on, when I was twenty, and spent much of my time at too young an age thinking about the past and regret. By then I was living on my own in an apartment where anyone I wished could have visited me—Tony could have come dressed in any iridescence of his choice, but he didn't, nor anyone like him. My brother was finishing high school by that time, and I saw him only on my infrequent visits home, and even then we rarely talked.

In fact, I didn't look at him closely again until years later, at a family reunion at Silver Lake, when he was married and had a son of his own. By then the efficiency cabins had been replaced by a clubhouse and the lake was too polluted for swimming. My brother was sitting in a lawn chair facing the beach, discussing his conservative views on race with a cousin of ours from Cleveland.

"I know it's not in style to admit it, but blacks always scared me, " he said. "When I was little, I even had nightmares about them. Once I dreamed that one was standing at the top of Loretta's steps."

He looked over appreciatively to where I was sitting alone

eating a bowl of ice cream, pretending to be totally self-obsessed. Of course, between that night in the car and the one on the steps, there had been dozens of other incidents my brother must have clearly remembered, but I had no idea what he had concluded from them. I could not imagine this, even remotely, so I continued to eat with lowered eyes and allowed him to observe me at his leisure, to think his own thoughts.

Toward the Ocean

EACH year around February my father began wearing a pained look when he shoveled the walk; I'd come upon my mother standing trapped on ice in her gripless high-heeled boots, unable to either proceed or back up. Stuck in our early-American house, our collective smells—my father's cigarette smoke, my mother's Aqua Net hairspray, the vile, bitter concoctions that I used to clear my face, straighten my hair—converged in the overheated rooms where we were trapped, cursed, unable even to hibernate.

I hated winter, partly, as I grew older, because of what it did to how I looked; my naturally curly hair fell straight, my skin turned pasty and rough. I believed that I looked even chubbier than usual in woolen plaids and mohair sweaters, which, stylish or not, itched and vexed me. I personally would have preferred to hide out until spring. We had enough provisions in our mini-fallout shelter in the basement to last quite a while. My mother had already stockpiled a variety of bargain canned goods that we never ate otherwise: round Irish potatoes, succotash, Harvard beets, those squishy, pale canned peas. The idea of having to eat them—as the idea of anything difficult—was thrilling to me. But there were no bombs in our neighborhood during those years to force us underground, and instead of hibernating, we began a yearly migration to Florida.

This escape from the bitterness of winter was

unlike any previous behavior of my parents, who in other realms never suggested that escape was either acceptable or possible. I grew up to a backdrop of chronic complaining, automatic and mostly female, over conditions that nothing could be done, perhaps should be done, about. The weather—too hot, humid, wet— was often featured in these harangues. Others were much more personal, involving husbands who disappointed, bodies that fell disloyally ill, diets that didn't work—ever. I heard: "What are you going to do? It's in the good Lord's hands." Or, more bitterly: "He cooked his own goose." "She made her own bed."

Accustomed to this, I found it remarkable that we were allowed to escape the trials of winter for a few weeks each season. The idea was not a natural one, but had been planted in my parents' heads after the free trip that my father won to Hollywood, Florida, when I was twelve. My brother and I were left behind with my grandmother on that trip, Mutual of Omaha being disinclined to finance children, but my parents returned parboiled and younger looking, with Polaroids of beaches and sea gulls, tales of record February temperatures and seafood platters. I was told that it took only one day, one brief twenty-four hours of a winter day that would surely be eventless at home, to drive as if in a dream to warmer regions. To move in the family car, our personal capsule, the backseat of which I found more comforting than any nook or cranny at home, from slick streets and gray slush into tropical heaven—"Yes, please," I exclaimed the first instant I heard of it. "Please let's go."

But I had to wait nearly two years from first hearing about this magic before they actually managed to take me along; my brother was still too young and had to remain behind with my grandmother. My parents were perhaps aware by then that it was unwise to tell me about anything that was possible but for which I had to wait. Waiting was not a notion that suited me, and I harassed them constantly during those years, at the same time as I kept a vigilant eye on bathing suits that might make me alluring, seafood dishes I might have the opportunity to taste, beach hairdos I might try. With one dreamy eye in beauty magazines, a critical one on my own body, I tried to imagine myself in an older, more sophisticated version, oiled and bronzed on some white beach, secluded except for several lifeguards who were pulled, as if by the tide, to gravitate worshipfully around me.

During this rather too long wait, other things were changing quickly; I was no longer a child. By the time we actually departed, the year I was fourteen, my eye, previously turned outward, looking, looking, was now focused exclusively on myself. In every rearview mirror, powder compact, shop window where I could position myself, I studied my reflection.

NO Route 75 then, we took back roads through Kentucky, Tennessee, Georgia, roads that spun past the backyards of Appalachia, where children sat near rusted garbage cans, and women, arms stretched, hung up bluejeans with holes in the rump. Old women positioned themselves south in wheelchairs on sparse lawns to catch the healing sun. Chain gangs—black men, silver chains—clanged along the meridian in Georgia, picking up litter with sharp-tipped stakes. Why didn't they stab the wardens, I wondered. Everything I saw I took in through my new self-absorbent tissues: What if we lived in a house like that, what if I were anchored with chains, how would I feel if I ever managed to be so old? My parents commented on none of this; in the front seat, their eyes seemed mesmerized by the black, endless road. And by the hour the heater in my father's Chevy was turned gradually lower, and we stripped off yet another layer of clothes. By the time we reached southern Georgia and stopped for a middle-of-the-night breakfast (prompted by me: "We haven't eaten for two whole states!"), we walked out into a world so balmy it was already like seawater.

My mother didn't approve of our stop, Truck City, a large

neon complex of gas pumps, a hotel, and a sprawling restaurant, but my father and I shared the conviction that men who drove in semis all day knew the best places to eat at night. We were the only car parked between the rows of towering tractor-trailers, into which I was dying to peek, sure the drivers were all sleeping with blond women who were not their wives. Once inside, my mother would not allow me to order what I wanted, the hefty trucker's special: six eggs any way you wanted them, a stack of pancakes, your choice of breakfast meats. She had her typical boring choice (two poached, dry toast), while my father and I were as exotic with fried meats and grits and gravy as we felt possible without gaining her disapproval.

Later she made me accompany her to the ladies' bathroom, where she instructed me to cover the seat with layers of toilet paper and then to squat, not sit. I disobeyed in the privacy of my stall—she couldn't tell me how to do everything—then wandered out to look at my dazed face in the mirror. It had been one of the few nights I could ever remember when I had been permitted *not* to sleep, and I saw immediately what it did. I looked haggard, as if some older, lurking self had peeked out to greet me. My mother only looked at herself briefly from the distance of her stall door, avoiding her reflection up close, as I noticed most older women did. I moved off as soon as she advanced close enough to brush her teeth, not liking to see us together, trapped, afraid of our resemblance.

Because my father and I were both groggy from overeating, my mother was forced to drive after that, something that she did frequently at home, but which she claimed became exceedingly difficult late at night, on highways, out of town. Because she braked so regularly and swerved at so many imaginary obstacles, my father and I were forced to remain awake, white-lipped, as if there were something we could do. After ninety painful miles of this, a suggestion of mine was surprisingly honored.

"Mom," I said. "Please let Dad drive."

Sure enough, as soon as my father moved into the seat, there was calm again; I did not like to think that this was simply because he was a man.

My mother and I snored, according to my father, for the next several hours (I knew my mother snored, but was hurt and vaguely embarrassed that I did also), and I dreamed of finding a pile of rubies in a discarded box and paying someone—a man again, but who?—to make them into a tiara. I did not know what my mother dreamed; she claimed not to, although I didn't believe her. An old joke of my father's was a dream she once had in which she cried out for someone named Jim.

"Oh, Jim, Jim" my father mocked.

"I never did!" she flared.

My father honked once, in exaltation, when we crossed the Florida border, but I only stirred briefly, still intent on my tiara and where exactly I was going to wear it. My mother woke then for good; in the top layer of my dreaming, I could hear her movements—her sniff, the rustling of unwrapping gum, the opening of her lipstick tube (Cinnamon Fire, but why did she need lipstick now?). I was the only one who experienced the complete thrill of waking up to open windows and the fringe of palms canopying the road, the one who when she finally sat up could taste salt, and saw, all at once, the distant glitter of water. To see the ocean, having never seen it—I briefly forgot even myself.

My mother, still loving me after all, made my father drive directly to the beach. They stayed in the car while I got out and walked down the sand in the beam of their protective headlights. I felt an old regard for them when they didn't honk the horn or hurry me along, letting me turn back in my own time to the safety of their waiting heads, silhouetted in the car. I had goose bumps, usually reserved for love scenes in movies and lyrics of songs, as I walked back to the car. But the bumps disappeared when we began driving again. I felt slightly carsick from sitting in the backseat, from my father's cigarette smoke and the constant radio blathering on—it seemed my parents would listen to anything.

Now that I had actually seen the ocean, I wanted to be near it, to be in it, immediately, but our final destination, the Sea Sand Hotel, took another hour and was a disappointment, to put it mildly. One small, drab room with shut windows that had trapped the lingering scents of the past occupant, who must have been a monumental smoker. My mother brandished disinfectant spray while my father unpacked in his methodical, unnerving way. I couldn't bear the thought of the three of us sleeping in this cheap room with its weak lights and filthy tweed chairs. But then I remembered—the ocean—and rushed out in my stiff new bathing suit, white as an embryo, to the sand.

As the days passed, life in our small room took on a back-home regularity, even with heaven right outside. My mother still got up early and woke both of us up—with the "Today Show" and the clink of her spoon (brought from home) in her coffee cup (brought also), with her toilet flushing and disapproving sniffs.

"Can't you sleep a little later, it's vacation," I grumbled when her noise forced me out of bed, but I really didn't mind. Even by 8:00 the sun was blazing through the venetian blinds, beckoning me. I ignored my mother's warnings about the severity of the sun and basked in it from early morning till nearly dusk, not burning as she smugly predicted (she burned), but staggering in each afternoon the hue of an increasingly darker race. I couldn't believe the colors I turned, from pink to gold, to a dark, rich brown. I'd never had my appearance so drastically altered: shut in the tiny bathroom with the heat lamp on, I surveyed my striped body with pride and amazement, thinking of adjectives that might be used to describe me. Since my parents went out only cautiously, my mother with an umbrella and lotions and sun hats, we looked like a multiracial family when we went to dinner each evening at the Fisherman's Wharf; people actually turned to look at us— at me, I thought triumphantly!

On our fourth night out, I admired myself in the window near our table, pretending to stare at scenery I was bored with already, my mother, of course, catching my subterfuge.

"I don't think you should go out in the sun anymore," she said, watching me watch myself. "You're dark enough now."

I ignored her, continuing to look out the window, intent on catching the eye of a young man walking by. Ah, I did it! Now I wanted to do it again.

"You *are* black," my father said then, and I looked up in surprise to find that he really was studying me; he didn't often do that.

"Well, what else am I supposed to do? Lie on my cot in the room? Watch "Jeopardy" on television?" I felt bitter, even though they were financing every second of this vacation, every fried clam that I stuffed into my mouth.

"I'm just saying it's enough," my mother said in low tones. She was eating crab Louise supreme in an attempt to diet, since she looked so fat in her one-piece. "There are other things to do here, you know. There's Thomas Edison's house . . ."

I rolled my eyes and interrupted. "I am *not* going to see where a dead man used to live. You guys go. I'm almost fifteen years old, and I'm perfectly all right by myself."

That was the end of the conversation, and the next day, to my immense surprise, my parents called my bluff and left me alone.

"Are you sure you'll be OK?" my mother asked, giving me a five-dollar bill. "We probably won't be back until late."

I was sitting on the bed, filing my nails, trying to hide my delight. Completely alone, out of state!

"Yes, I'll be fine. I might even stay inside and read," I lied.

"All right. Well." My father jingled the change in his pocket, and then they were gone.

I watched between the venetian blinds as they pulled off, more excited than I'd ever been in my life. But once they'd disappeared, I was left in our stuffy room again with an overcast day outside. Where were all of the secret, forbidden things I was free to do now? My father hadn't even left behind any cigarettes that I could sneak. I turned on the TV and danced a moment, wildly, to the music on a soft-drink commercial; I put a quarter in the Magic Fingers and gyrated for a few minutes on the bed; I took off all my clothes and walked around with only my sandals, pretending I was a Caribbean prostitute. Well, that's it, I thought. I put on my bathing suit, grabbed my towel and beauty magazine, and went outside, my mind filling with typically depressing thoughts. Our last full day, and it was overcast, I thought gloomily, not giving the weather—or luck, or whatever—any credit for having been perfect the four days before. I lay on my stomach and read cuticle tips, the same old dieting advice (keep carrot sticks handy, drink plenty of water), hints for enhancing eyelash growth. Finally I sat up and pretended to be profoundly lost in the lap of the ocean, but I was really sizing up the boys who walked by. I thought that a particular one—a particular, extremely handsome one—had walked by me a number of times. He was like a magazine boy, perfect and blond and bronze; I'd had daydreams about such boys, but felt too much a misfit to actually attract one in reality.

But here he was, standing at the corner of my beach towel, which had instructions for mixed drinks printed on it—a gift from one of my father's clients. I straightened a leg to cover up a margarita recipe, afraid it might give the wrong impression, and continued to look at the ocean, sure he was hesitating near me only by coincidence. Perhaps he had lost something nearby.

"Are you a model?"

I looked up in surprise, then over my shoulder, where there was only a very old man in plaid shorts probing the sand for lost money. Surely he wasn't talking to him. I looked up again; he was speaking to me, all right.

"No. No, I'm not. I'm a . . ." What? "A student," I finished lamely.

"Well, you sure look like a model to me." The boy grinned, slipping down beside me. "I'm Jeff. Jeff Nicols, and I'm not a model either."

He gave me his hand, like an adult, which he may have been. I gave him my clammy paw, and he squeezed it, then placed it back on my lap, as if it weren't mine.

"You live around here?"

"No," I said again. Was this all I could say? ("Be upbeat, never negative with dates," my beauty magazines had warned.) "We're from Ohio. On vacation. My family and me."

"Oh." He smiled, looking me over. "I live in Fort Myers. Got my own apartment," he offered, unasked.

I nodded.

"It's real nice. Great stereo system. You like the Stones?"

I nodded again.

"You gotta hear them on this system. It'd blow your ears out," he said, as if this would be pleasurable.

We sat in silence then, my mind as flat as a pane of glass.

"So, do you want to see it?" he asked suddenly, making me jump.

"What?"

"My apartment. We could go there later tonight. That is, if your parents don't mind."

My parents. It felt like a slap in the face. If I resembled a model, surely parents were of little consequence.

"Oh, no. I come and go as I please," I said, trying hard to smile.

"Great!" He jumped to his feet. "Why don't I come back here and pick you up at about seven."

"OK, that's fine."

He grinned again, then began sprinting down the beach, like

the apparition I was sure he must have been. It was only when he had been reduced to a blond pinpoint on the horizon that I realized he had not even asked for my name.

I had five hours. I spent almost two of them agonizing over makeup at the Rexall several blocks from our hotel; then back onto the beach for another hour, in case there were a few more sunrays I might catch. I spent another half hour in the hotel room with diarrhea, then back to the Rexall, where, counting change, I bought a bottle of Kaopectate, drinking half of it down. That left an hour and a half for getting ready. I tried on every outfit that I'd brought in my suitcase, then even tried on what my mother'd brought along. My skin was covered with a sheen of sweat as I worked away on my face. A model, I thought. Ha! I could never have done this kind of thing every day.

Finally it was time: I had altered as much of myself as possible, and my parents still had not arrived. I couldn't think of a convincing lie to write in a note, so I simply left, after turning out the lights to the disorder I'd left behind.

Jeff was waiting for me on the beach, perfect in duck trousers and a pink oxford cloth shirt. When he smiled upon seeing me, I thought instantly: Love, this is it.

"Hi. You look good enough to eat," he said, putting his arm around me and leading me to his car nearby, while I numbly filed away this compliment to savor later, like leftover pizza. He drove to a liquor store and left me waiting with the kind of passive, self-satisfied expression I'd seen on female passengers all my life until he returned with a bottle of wine.

"Chablis," he said, pulling me close. "Pink." And then he kissed me on the mouth.

Then we were in his apartment, all cushions and orange crates, and he was flipping on the stereo and pouring us wine—all pretenses, I knew, all preliminaries. I sat for a while on a lumpy sofa that was covered with a sheet, then went into the bathroom to bide my time and stare at my hot, puzzled face.

"Under my thumb," Jeff was singing happily when I came out. I saw that he had already chainlocked the door and dimmed the lights. Now he pulled the shades and lit a candle in a wine bottle. Well, here he comes, I thought as he approached me on the couch.

"So, what do you think? About the apartment," he asked, snuggling up beside me.

"Oh, it's nice. Real nice."

"Yeah, I like it. Great stereo system, huh?"

"Yeah, real great."

And that was it, as far as conversation went. Then he was on me, over me, around me, arms, lips, warm, wet. It all went on for an amazing length of time. I surfaced now and then, like a drowning swimmer, to notice that the hands on his illuminated clock had moved drastically: 8:00, 9:00. My parents flitted in and out of my mind, a world away; then Jeff was back again.

Finally, when he had ground me into the sheets of the couch and unbuttoned most of my clothing, he surfaced himself, breathing heavily, looking intently into my face. I swallowed and blinked back. Well? I wanted to say.

"Uh, have you taken anything . . . you know, today," he asked.

Baffled, I continued to look at him, unsure of what he meant. "Well, I had a little Kaopectate earlier," I said.

He looked at me even more closely. "Exactly how old are you . . ."

"Loretta," I said.

He sat up, away from me. "Yeah, Loretta. How old are you exactly."

"Well, fourteen. And a half, really. My birthday's in . . ."

"Fourteen!" He almost screamed it, and I sat up fully myself. Oh, God, it had all gone wrong, just as I'd feared. He got up, zipped his pants—how had they become unzipped, I thought, horrified: I hadn't done that—poured himself more wine and took it into the bathroom, where I thought I heard him chuckle. When he came back out, I had straightened myself as much as I could without a mirror and stood waiting.

"Is something wrong?" I asked.

"Wrong? No, no. Nothing's wrong. I just remembered this appointment I've got at ten, and I've really got to get going."

"Going?" I repeated stupidly.

"Yeah, going. Listen, Loretta, maybe I'll call you at your hotel sometime, and we can get together for a drink again."

He was all car keys and combs and belt buckles as he pushed me out the door. I'd written down my address for him earlier in the hotel room, but I couldn't find it now in the clutter of new makeup in my purse. Defeated, I walked to the passenger side of the car, but it was locked. I stood waiting patiently as Jeff got in the other side, started the engine, and turned on the radio. He looked over at me after he'd combed his hair again in the rear-view mirror and finally rolled down the window.

"Loretta, I'm in kind of a rush, so I won't be able to take you home. You don't mind walking, do you?"

Walking! I looked around wildly. "I don't even know where I am," I cried as he began rolling up the window again.

"Sure you do. Your hotel's on the beach. Just walk south. Toward the ocean." And then he was gone.

It was miles away; I knew that before I even began. I'd spent the last of my money on Kaopectate, so I couldn't call a cab even if I'd known how. "You've made your own bed, you've made your own bed," female voices from Ohio chanted, far away. I was perfectly ready to get into it; even the lumpy cot at the Sea Sand seemed beckoning as I trudged along.

Finally, a long while later, at approximately the same hour as I'd first seen it and from nearly the same angle, the ocean appeared in front of me. I approached it eagerly, and once on the beach, dropped my purse. Please, I prayed, looking out, let me feel that way again.

I closed my eyes, then opened them; I breathed deeply; I stared. But all I could think was that my feet hurt and that I had to pee badly and that my mother would be waiting, worried, sharp-eyed— she would discern instantly what had happened.

To see the ocean, having never seen it. I picked up my purse and walked on, telling myself that I was practically there.

PART II

◆

Sugar Street

Specialists

THAT summer my mother sent me to the dermatologist, Dr. Turner, for what she called a preventive checkup against acne. My mother never had acne herself, but she saw the ravages all around her— in my classmates, those poor blighted girls who people said "might" have been pretty if their faces had not been marked with scars. My mother felt especially sorry for the girls, but there were boys who were marked also. They were called "crater face" and "sausage skin;" my mother did not plan on having me called that. Although I had few pimples at the time, Dr. Turner gave me an ultraviolet treatment—which several years later was discovered to be not only useless but dangerous—two tubes of a strong ointment named Fostril that caused red, scaldlike patches whenever I used it, and a supply of zinc and vitamin A.

Examining pustules and boils seemed a mournful profession to me, and indeed Dr. Turner later shot himself, when I was in college, many years after this visit. I often saw his wife in Gregg's, both before his death and after, a sleek faced woman who looked as if her skin had been bound and pulled behind her neck like a scarf. Her youthful look, year after year, was shocking and disturbing, and people assumed that Dr. Turner had arranged a series of facelifts for her before his death.

My appearance until that year had been something my mother worried about on my behalf; she not only offered me advice on what to wear, she even sewed for me. She legislated my hairstyle, my shoes; I was her singular creation. But this changed forever with my visits to Dr. Turner and the sudden awareness that my looks required both medical intervention and vigilance. I became obsessed with viewing myself in dressing-room mirrors, where I was thrown into unhappy triplicate, every dimension of myself revealed. I had not known, or really ever wanted to know, how I looked at a ninety-degree angle; seeing myself like this changed everything. I never again put on a pair of pants or shorts or culottes without wondering how my rear end looked in them, from behind. With the help of older, more experienced girls, I learned to mask my face in orange liquids and glittered powders that finally produced the pimples that had been expected all along.

Throughout all this, my mother continued to plot for my prettiness. After all, she must have reasoned, what else was there to hope for me? Her own dreams, loose and lost as they were, had evidently come to naught. She was a suburban housewife, hemmed in by her wall-to-wall carpet, the boundaries of her vast, scuffed tile. That she had once planned to be a singer, a piano player, a star on the clarinet, were all secret, useless passions, now as gone as her youth. When they raised up unexpectedly, when she began to sing in the car during trips to Silver Lake, such yearning, hopeful tunes as "Meet Me in St. Louis" or "But Not for Me," I would hang my head out of the window and let the air obliterate her sound, or cringe until someone—my father, my brother— asked her to please shut up. She had a thrilling soprano there was no place for; it soared embarrassingly over the congregation when she sang at church, too exuberant for Methodist hymns. If she sang in the yard as she hung up clothes, standing between walls of whipping sheets, neighbors thought she was showing off. She could not sing at the living-room piano because it was in competition with the TV, which my brother and I had running so continually that it gave off a burning, electrical smell. We much preferred watching Lucy and Ethel sneak into the Copacabana to sabotage one of Ricky's rehearsals than to hear her sing. She was our mother—what did she think she was doing?

As I grew older, I caught her reading romances that she bought at the grocery when I wasn't along—books called *Crystal Dreams* or *Twilight Embrace*. I sometimes read them when she was at her club or out to eat with my father; they featured heroines with melting bones and swollen throats. One sentence appeared with little variation near the end of these books, after the heroine fought against the man who was plotting for her affection: *She saw that it was useless to resist*. To resist what? I wondered. And why was it useless?

I heard my mother groan with disgust over these books, but noted that she continued buying them and made a big production of keeping them from me.

"They'll just fill your head with more nonsense than is already there," she'd say.

"Then why do you read them?"

"I don't read them—I—they amuse me," she answered, looking at me as she often did then, regretfully.

By that time I had entered my fifteenth year and suffered the demise of my romance with our paperboy, who had kissed me for many weeks through the screen door, leaving my lips crisscrossed and chapped. I was going to another specialist by then, a child psychologist named Dr. Ira Erwin, who my parents had sent me to because I was seeing a black boy named Luther. The only reason my mother knew about Luther at all was because she listened at the bottom of the steps when I phoned him each night— 228-9286, a number I still remember by heart. My mother deciphered these digits by the number of clicks as I dialed, then gave them to my father, who had, as one of his few perks in the insurance industry, access to a cross-city phone directory. He looked up the number and thereby discovered Luther, or rather Luther's family, Biggs, 22 East Sugar Street. The address and last name were singular evidence in our town that Luther was black, poor, and not someone I was allowed to communicate with even by phone. If they had only known the rest. At least my mother had been spared the sight of me teasing my hair between geometry and gym class, frantically outlining my lids, and painting my mouth into a target for the brief hallway interlude I had with Luther each day, when I simpered down the hall pretending not to look for him. He also pretended, much better than I, not to look for me, and later on I saw that he probably wasn't, that he stood there leaning against the bulletin board, his lovely, loose brown body perfectly natural, for whatever fate brought his way.

"Say, girl, you're looking good. You going to the game?"

"I think so."

"Who with?"

"Some friends."

"What's his name?"

(Flustered). "Not a guy."

"You sure?"

"Yes, I'm sure."

"All right then. I'll be seeing you."

This was all there was, but these conversations, especially the constant suggestion of deception on my part, thrilled and confused me. My mother knew nothing about this, but perhaps she had imagined enough to send me to Dr. Erwin, who tried to incite me to candor regarding my relationship with Luther.

"This Luther, how did you meet him?"

"In school."

"He's a sophomore too, or older?"

"Older."

"How much older?"

"Two years."

Dr. Erwin looked narrowly at a piece of paper that had information he must have already known: my name, my address, the presenting problem.

"Your parents, you know, are quite worried about the possibility of any relationship with this boy. Why do you think that is?"

"You know why. He's black."

"Do you think that's all?"

"Most of it."

"I think they're more worried about any sexual involvement that may develop with this Luther. He is older, and in his cultural milieu, as I'm sure you know, these kind of things . . ."

Sexual involvement—I knew he was right, and of course my parents had every reason to worry, but I did not tell Dr. Erwin that it was a bit too late. I never disclosed anything of the truth during the rest of our visit; in fact, I refused to go back to him at all, as I refused to do many things. How could I have explained Luther Biggs to him or to anybody? How this boy—man—with his broken black plastic glasses and suede shirts and strange, vegetable breath, had so captured my imagination? Surely part of it was that he was forbidden, always over there—on the other side of the cafeteria, the other side of the tracks, the other side of the sidewalk, with his laughing, white-toothed friends and their lilting, jeering talk. Who could have resisted him? Not many, evidently, because I quickly learned that I was one of many white girls who received Luther's notes—stuck somewhere in the middle of a civics book, say near judicial systems or parliamentary government—notes that I received dozens of times before Luther actually had me. For a long while our affair was carried on this way, slights and misunderstandings beginning and ending through the communiqués we passed each other in the halls:

"Girl, you know I don't care nothing for Marcia Davies, that old skinny redhead. She ain't nothing compared to you. I'm still waiting for you to come over and see me (smile). When are you gonna make up your mind?"

I had already made up my mind, of course; it was simply a matter of timing, or perhaps courage is a better word. I was perfectly content to continue our intrigue in the hallways, to talk to Luther late at night, listening to his syrupy voice tell me what he would do when he finally got me over to 22 East Sugar Street. The truth was, I would rather have continued this way. But I had competition, and did not ever really believe that he had been talking to Marcia Davies only for her math notes. I saw that there were plenty of white girls, especially then, in the sixties, who would take up Luther instantly on his proposals, and probably already had.

Why did I feel I had to bother to compete? Surely this was a question that Dr. Erwin would have asked me had I continued going to him, but it was not one my mother would have bothered with, for example, having read, however scornfully, enough of her romance magazines. The truth was that I wanted to keep that attention, that singular, pointed, and flattering focus, on myself. And I knew even then that the paperboy and his type would not be enough for me; at fifteen I suddenly and fiercely wanted more.

What did I want? Luther actually asked me that later when he finally had me on Sugar Street, after I had lain in a humiliating crouch in the back of his Chevy as we passed through neighborhoods where it mattered if I was seen. He did not realize what an absurd question it was to ask at that time of someone like me. We were in his bedroom after all, one of many firsts. And in the end I could not tell Luther what it was I wanted, because he was talking about desires of a physical nature, and mine were too achingly new and unnameable in that attic bedroom where he undressed me only partially, as if he might have to quickly leave the vicinity, and made what I knew they referred to as love. He seemed more concerned later that I may have stretched out his knit shirt by pulling on him in what he imagined my passion, what I knew as my pain. He thought I was lost in it, staring at the ceiling, but I was really thinking of those love stories I had sneaked from my mother, of the italicized words, those improbable endings I must have believed in somehow: *And in his arms, she saw that reality had finally surpassed her fondest dreams.*

The breadth of Luther's conquests became clear to me later, as I learned that he not only had a number of white girls, all vying for his affection, but a number of infinitely sassy, wise, and more experienced black ones. I came to dread my time in the halls between classes, when I would invariably turn a corner and find him in some alcove talking to another girl. There were so many of us, it occurred to me then—so many of us, wan and yearning so early for love. And indeed there were enough that Luther's specific interest in me sometimes foundered; his notes were often one-line instructions of where to meet him, when not to call.

"I told you I had basketball practice on Fridays, so don't be calling and bothering Netty."

I was especially stung by this insinuation—that I might bother his sister, who was an unwilling observer of our trysts in her house. What she must have thought of me in my pink wool skirts rolled up at the waistband, of my hair spray and cologned mohair sweaters, trailing after her brother like a heartsick dog.

Sometimes I heard her rustling near the bathroom door when I was inside, fixing myself after Luther had unceremoniously mussed me up, and wondered how she really felt about my intrusion, about this white girl sequestered in her toilet, full of the sperm of her family. Occasionally she was the only person I reached when I telephoned Luther's number each night, since for unexplained reasons he sometimes stayed at his mother's house. Netty answered the phone with the same drawling lack of expectation I heard in my mother's voice. Had Dr. Erwin known, he would have surely called this ironic: that by the time my mother brought herself to the bottom of my steps to copy those digits, I was only talking to another woman, not much different than she was, but many neighborhoods away.

Sugar Street

BY that night I was a common visitor at Netty Biggs' house as the white girlfriend of her younger brother Luther, and was already her admirer. She was a slow-moving, big-laughing black woman, who always held up the grocery line counting penny rolls and quarters, while her son Andre grabbed Chiclets behind her. No one else in my family would have even noticed her existence, yet here I was, knowing all about her—as much as could be known from sitting on her plush, often repossessed furniture, as much as could be gathered from eating out of her fragrant pots, where one thing cooked into the next. "How you doin'?" she asked the first day I met her, and this was often all she said to me later on.

Luther and I went to Netty's house on Sugar Street because we had no money and no place else to go. All we possessed between the two of us was our love and his rusted Chevy, with its bald tires and less than a quarter-tank of gas. By the time he picked me up a block from my house, in front of the TV station on the corner of Rosewood and Rice, it would be quarter after six, an hour when my family, having already consumed and partly digested a meal of meat loaf or baked chicken or hamburger patties, had settled down to watch Chuck Ferris, wearing an ascot, deliver the local news. After hog and grain prices and before the weather forecast—mostly overcast, usually forty-five—came the most exciting part of the report, the petty crimes and domestic squabbles in the black part of our town, where Netty Biggs lived and where I escaped, my mouth full of fabricated library visits and friends I did not have, as my family belched and yawned and turned up the heat.

Standing on the corner waiting for Luther, I was at an exact midpoint between my parents' mortgaged aluminum-sided house, full of cold remedies and throw rugs, and the great TV tower of WYMA, which blinked its red light directly onto my face the nights I slept crooked on my bed. When I was younger, I imagined that this light could be seen from distant places, that it connected us, in our smallness, with something else, large. But I was wrong; with its dim wattage and low frequency, the station barely encompassed our town and shut down nightly at nine. Even so, there were frequent lapses—high-pitched tests of the Emergency Broadcasting System that caused the neighborhood beagles and poodles and dachshunds to arch their necks and howl, times when the set went inexplicably blank and a sign appeared, pleading PLEASE STAND BY. Since it was the only station we received, my family obeyed. But as I grew older, I wished neither to stand still nor by. Not when my father listed his endless, arbitrary rules to me—rules he was too dim to know that I had already, long ago, ignored—nor when my mother, her mouth full of straight pins, tried to mark neat hems on the skirts that I hitched up at the waistband as soon as I left the house.

It was a dark thrill that my family knew so little about my life, that they did not even have the imagination to forbid what I was doing. "Don't go out with a Negro," they had said. But, "Do not sit on the toilet of an unmarried black mother or let her sweet-smelling brother unbutton your drip-dry blouse"—no, such specific words, such wild warnings would not have entered their mild minds. They did not know that the only relief I ever felt was when I opened the door to Luther's Chevy, stepped into the scent of gasoline and hair oil and cigarette smoke, all mingled at the high temperature of the car's strong heater; that my only freedom was when he drove us across the railroad tracks to a region where no one else in my family had ever been, would ever go.

I had driven with and lain beside and held on to parts of Luther as autumn turned to winter; I was sixteen, and if we could find a place—and I could keep his interest—I thought that we might do these things forever. But for now, we had to see if time would change things, and we waited on Sugar Street. This particular night was our one-month anniversary, a fact I secretly cherished as Luther drove me over the railroad tracks, past Lee's BBQ and the Dairy Dip Drive-In, where the waitresses were all rumored to have gonorrhea. We drove by Park's Funeral Home, with its ancient illuminated clock that always said 6:17, a time I eventually began to associate with death; past Elliott's drugstore, where you could buy quinine and other concoctions that would bring on a missed period; and finally we were on Sugar Street, and I rolled down the window and let the tart air roll in.

When we reached Netty's house, I followed Luther through the open door and into the living room, where Andre was spelling words with Fruit Loops in front of Chuck Ferris, who was stumbling over the weather—a low-pressure system was on its way, he was saying, pointing to our town, a highlighted speck in the northwestern corner of Ohio.

"Do we have to watch this?" I asked Luther, who had sunk down with Andre on the floor. He spelled boot with the cereal, then shrugged his shoulders, looking up at me, the way he always looked up at me, with amusement and annoyance and—I hoped—enormous love. "Loretta," he said when he was finished looking, "what else do you think is on?"

I threw down my purse and wandered into the kitchen, picking up a chicken wing, long cold. One month, I was thinking, and not even a kiss or a card. I had bought a wallet in brown vinyl—for his rubbers and dollar bills and photographs of Andre—that was wrapped in tissue paper in my purse in case he suddenly

surprised me, but I saw that he would not. All he did was turn
up Chuck Ferris, so his voice floated into the kitchen, full of bad
news, forcing me into the bathroom, where I sat down on the
closed stool and watched Netty Biggs preparing herself for the
night: first lighting a Kool, which she placed, burning yellow,
on the edge of the sink, then arranging on top of her scruffy hair
a magnificent blue-black coil that she twisted and twined and
poked with pins.

"Where are you goin'?" I asked when she was at a stage where
I thought she could talk.

"Club 21, Ladies' Night. You oughta get Luther to take you
sometime. You know Sam and Dave?" she asked, looking at me
closely.

I nodded.

"Well, they'll be there tonight."

I fell silent then, although I wanted to ask who she was going
to meet—not to be nosy, just out of curiosity. I had no sister of
my own and often coveted one, simply to ask such questions as
this. I wondered where Netty Biggs went with the men she knew,
since I had never seen one of them in her house. Although she
sometimes told stories featuring one of them to Luther, they
remained faceless characters with their fascinating names—Otis
and Butterbean and Ingram; they blew the horns of dark cars at
nine-thirty each night, and I sometimes thought I smelled their
sperm on her later, when we passed in the hall.

I watched in silent admiration as Netty Biggs smoked the rest
of her Kool and adhered her eyelashes and puffed her face with
a dark powder that was the shade of the earth I once saw when
my family visited relatives in Georgia. Here was a woman who
stood all day on concrete floors welding radio parts, then drove
home to cook pork in a pot and wipe the nose of her son. Then
she coiled a wig on her head and went out to hear Sam and
Dave, probably dancing the way I'd seen her do in the kitchen,

gyrating slowly, as if underwater, smoking a cigarette and drinking down a shot glass of gin.

I couldn't imagine that I would do any of these things, ever; as far as I knew, the way things were might just be the way they'd always remain. After Netty left the bathroom, I closed the door and stared a long time at my face, trying to imagine myself in middle, then old age, still driving with Luther across the railroad tracks, up Sugar Street. But then I saw how many other things would have changed. My parents would have died, leaving me no household to repudiate, no need for a corner to wait on. Even the old Chevy Luther and I rode in could not make it much longer, and what about him? In a year he would be out of school, at some job that would probably involve his fingers—I knew he had talent in them from the way they had worked on me—but he had never mentioned marriage or any date further away than the next week. And Netty Biggs—surely at some point she would not be doing this. Surely someday she would be too worn or arthritic or jaded to put on a wig and twist her hips, to open her door to me or her arms to another man and his baby.

Not wanting to think these things, I thought them anyway, looking at my pale and young and uncertain face. Then I turned off the light and padded into the doorway of Netty's bedroom, just in time to see her look up and smile at me as she fastened onto herself a pair of false hips.

White Girls

ANNIE BIGGS watches her son Luther walk in the door and thinks that since he began seeing white girls, they have drifted apart. She finds it hard to remember just when this started—the past year has been confusing. Her husband, Horace, died a week after Malcolm X, and then Luther began growing his hair. It had once been so short that he had not even combed it; now his space in the bathroom is crowded with special brushes, creams. Long hair does not bother Annie as much as it does other mothers she knows. She sees more than she mentions; she personally wears a wig. But lately she feels his manhood between them like some strange, third presence, muting what had once been implicit—that he was above all her son.

Luther, who is eighteen, has always had girlfriends. Just like her husband, Horace, he seems to attract women. (She does not mourn Horace's death and never really has. It does not erase the distinct memory that he was never very kind.) She found so many hairpins in Horace's backseat during their many years of marriage that she developed a certain philosophical distance. "He's just being a man," she said.

But it took a long while for her to come to this point. When she was seventeen and they were first married and moved north from Alabama, she was completely at his mercy; it was like being with her father. She was a bowlegged girl with buck teeth and wild eyes, and the first gift Horace gave her was a pageboy wig from Japan. Annie wore it with some awe and because her new husband was so insistent. He said her own hair made her look like a boy, but Annie knew even then, as she learned to comb the straight, blue-black locks, that this wasn't exactly what he meant. But she somehow kept faith in her husband until she lost her first child, a girl two weeks old with a head like a teardrop, whom she had alternately christened Temple, Louise, and Tiffany the day she died. Annie found out a month before her birth that Horace was having an affair with a waitress, and later saw for herself when she followed him downtown: the woman was white and had red tinted hair and a face like a horse. Annie watched as Horace rushed to open the door and the woman snuggled up closely beside him. Later that night when he didn't come home, she threw her wig in the garbage, broke the cups from her only set of china, and crawled into bed and cried. It was the last emotional excess she allowed herself either in public or private. But she reclaimed her wig the next day, because she was too self-conscious without it, and let friends inform her about the affair, although she had stopped wanting to know. The waitress was a divorcée from Detroit. Horace had already bought her a fox jacket and a cultured-pearl ring. Annie lay awake some nights thinking of him spraying in the waitress the same seed that had caused her own child, but she never let on that she knew, and after the baby was born said she did not want to be told anymore. Still, over the years she lived in this unnamed woman's presence, carried in her letters from the mailbox, washed her hair from Horace's shirts. With some effort she reduced her curiosity to what that long, peach hair must have felt like, why she had ever dyed it that particular shade.

Horace was so absorbed in his affair that he paid little attention to the baby and was annoyed when Annie wanted to spend money for a funeral. He assumed that she would give in to his wishes, but Annie, dressed in black wool and matured during their marriage to her full five-foot-nine, found him at the pool hall and laid down the law, made him drive to the bank and draw out all the money she needed. (That funeral more than any other had broken her heart: sweetheart roses and a casket tiny as a crib. Tiffany was so small you could hardly find her, nestled like a seed in the satin.) After that, Horace did what she asked, although she asked for very little. There were just a few points of respect that she insisted upon. "Let me know if you're not coming home for dinner so I don't stand like a fool fixing it. If you have to lay with every woman in town, do me a favor and avoid my friends. When I want to go back to Alabama, you buy the ticket—you brought me here. Stay out of my purse, bring me your paycheck, and give me another child if I ever want one."

Horace did these things, and after that they rarely argued, but it was all the rest he didn't do that she never would have asked for. He forgot her birthday (she noticed her friend Gloria's husband bought her a new suede jacket every year), never came home and suggested taking her to dinner, never stole up behind and kissed her on the ear. Their lovemaking was like the fighting that they never did out loud: she would refuse; he would insist. She had broken so many bedroom lamps that the room finally remained dark. Horace's life was so separate from hers that she was sometimes surprised to see him walk into the house.

"Say," he would mutter, and throw down his car keys, then empty the rest of his pockets.

As Annie passed in and out of her twenties, then into her thirties, she focused away from herself, past the silence. She volunteered, worked part time at the hospital, and became recognized in the neighborhood as someone you could count on. She enjoyed doing things for people and knew she would be good with a child. But after Tiffany she put it out of her mind, until that year she missed all her periods and thought it was early menopause. She cried on the gynecologist's table, partly because she was scared of the instruments, partly from being happy.

"What are you gonna do with a baby at your age?" was all Horace said when she told him, but she overheard him comment later from the backyard, "Guess I ain't old yet." Neighbors stopped asking favors, and Annie spent her pregnancy in peaceful oblivion, knitting booties, watching TV movies, and gaining sixty-five pounds. Her aunt Lucille came from Alabama and delivered her daughter Netty in the bedroom. Seven years later, there was Luther.

LUTHER stops in front of her now and opens a can of beer. "So, Mama," he says, kissing her vacantly. "What's going on?"

He has been gone for the weekend and smells like a room of flowers, and she can tell by the bruised look of his lips that he has just finished making love.

"Not much, baby," she tells him. "Just doing my little stuff."

Luther walks into the living room and turns on the TV and stereo at the same time. This does not annoy her; he is her son, even though he looks just like Horace; his head was once buried inside her like an onion. When he first had girlfriends, she had felt slightly jealous, used to having his affection to herself. They were black girls from the neighborhood and nothing very serious, although she often heard the mattress squeaking above her. She went to her room out of courtesy when the girls came to visit. Luther had always done that—brought them to her like prizes— had never spent his life out in the streets like Horace. Sometimes she even made sandwiches and left them on the table, as she had for Santa Claus as a child. The girls had singsong names she could never remember and wore jangly bracelets as they held tightly to Luther's arm. He talked about them when there was trouble, but that was rare. (Unlike Horace, who brought out the worst in women. Early in their marriage women had honked and yelled in front of the house. This abruptly stopped when Annie went out in her pyjamas and kicked Horace squarely in the ass as he stood with his head inside a car.)

This hardly happened with Luther, although she could tell by the looks on their faces that these girls were frankly in love. Annie remembered this as an illness: cramps in her stomach, a swimming head. She noticed with pleasure that her son was somewhat kinder than Horace; he pulled out chairs now and then and had once even bought her a hothouse corsage. Still, she couldn't ignore the disdain he sometimes used with these girls, a disrespect that was both so oblique and familiar that she would have to leave the room at the memories it aroused.

Then, after Horace died, there was a long stretch when Luther didn't go out at all. He sat listlessly in front of the television, although she knew he wasn't watching. (Horace had died on the other side of town from coronary failure. Speculation in the street was predictable, and Luther seemed worried she would be hurt. "Listen," she told him. "I was married to your daddy twenty years. Long enough to know what he was and wasn't.")

It was after this that Luther let his hair grow and began seeing white girls. She thought he was growing his hair out of black pride: the introduction of white girls at this time slightly confused her. These girls often called him on the phone, something the black girls had rarely done. They had creamy voices that sounded antagonistic, and with some awkwardness Luther began to talk about them: Karen was rich, and he had eaten at her house and been served poached salmon; Vicki was an art student from Cleveland; Carol's father was a socialist and blacklisted during McCarthy. Annie found the idea of her son eating salmon in a white house—something she had never done—vaguely disturbing.

"How did they treat you?" she had asked, and he looked at her—first surprised, then sad—and said, "Good."

When the white girls came home with him, Luther left them

in the hallway. Annie wandered up, denying that it was more than curiosity. She said nothing to Luther, but she had her opinions. Karen tried to dress as if she were poor, which Annie found silly; Carol smoked cigarettes and dropped ashes on her rug. A few were so friendly that she could not help thinking they saw her as an important ally. Already one had called her Annie on the phone and asked if she knew where Luther had gone.

"Yes," Annie had answered. "But you'll have to find out from him."

She knew he had a reputation in the neighborhood because of the white girls, but she said it was his business. She also knew it had changed the way people treated her, noticed a few narrow looks when she went out to shop.

"Getting kind of classy, aren't you?" Willy the dry cleaner asked. "Saw a little blonde sitting in Luther's car."

"You should keep your nose out of other people's driveways," Annie said, and walked out.

Although she never encouraged them, Annie still had a small ring of male admirers, and Willy, who was one, smiled and let it go.

"Aw, Annie, let me in," he sometimes called through the window.

"Go take a shower," she yelled out. "I don't have time for that mess anymore." In her frequent dreams, she occasionally had a romantic one where she bounded down a flowered hill into the arms of a faceless lover. But the woman in these dreams was not really like her at all, and she sometimes joked about it with Luther.

"Momma, you don't have to dream about it," he said. But he had misunderstood—she had only meant to make him laugh. Such a laugh! He had teeth just like hers, even if his face was from Horace.

Still, by the way he hung around, she knew Luther sometimes felt guilty about leaving her. "Go on out," she always told him. "I got plenty to do on my own." She habituated the library, and from her bed had become the local expert on a number of topics. She had learned enough obstetrics when she was pregnant to know how to deliver a baby, and had done so on several occasions when the ambulance, reluctant to enter black neighborhoods, had been too late to help. She was fascinated by planets and particularly knowledgeable about Saturn. "Those rings are made of separate particles," she told Luther, "some as big as a house." She could identify local bird songs, read palms, and interpret dreams. It was true she was slowing down now, but Luther seemed to forget these things when he worried so much about her. In the last month, during his second spell of solitude, he had become even worse, and Annie came upon him on several occasions rummaging through boxes of his father's old things.

"What you got there?" she asked once when she found him reading a letter

"Nothing," he said quickly, but she could tell he was embarrassed.

He began to stay around the house in the evening, watching her closely, as if she were ill.

"Nothing's wrong with me except worrying about you worrying," she said. "What's the matter with you, son?"

That was three nights ago, and Luther had left the room, avoiding her eyes. Over the weekend she thought about it and decided that it must be over some girl; other matters had never affected him. She walks into the living room now, wiping her hands on a towel.

"Talk to me," she says to him. "Tell me what's wrong."

Luther looks at her, then turns away.

"It's this white girl," he says finally.

"Well," she says. "Why don't you tell me about it?"

"It's not like the others, Momma," he says. "That's why I haven't brought her around."

Annie rubs her hands on the towel again, although they've already dried, and stands looking out the window. Time has always tricked her; she could never get used to it. This is the same window she stood at when Luther was teething, cuddled up on the same couch, no bigger than her knee. She doesn't know what to say, but wishes she could hold him as she did then.

"What's her name?" she asks finally.

"Loretta," he says.

LATER that night Annie thinks it must be Loretta's silhouette she sees waiting in Luther's car when he runs into the house for a pack of cigarettes. He kisses Annie in the hallway as he backs out again, leaving on her cheek a smell from her youth that she cannot immediately place.

She watches his car pull past a street light that illuminates for an instant the high bone of the white girl's cheek. When they're gone, she says "gardenias," then picks from her dress the other thing Luther has left on her, a long, pale strand of that hair.

Homecoming

◆

I

NO matter how pretty or deserving you were prior to 1966, most black men in Union preferred the allure of whites. It was still a status symbol to have a blond head, however bleached, glisten from the front seat of your car, to have a long white leg, or a short, fat white one, extend itself from your door.

But it was different that year, partly due to the winds of the world, which blew belatedly that winter from the northeast, near Cleveland. Afro Sheen appeared next to skin bleachers in Elliott's Drugs, and James Brown sold out before the Beach Boys at Frank's Record Shop. White girls moved over to give space at bathroom mirrors and tried to mimic the hairstyle of Elaine Johnson, the town's first black homecoming queen. And eighteen-year-old Luther Biggs woke up one January morning beside a white girl in his sister Netty's house and wondered why he continued to waste his seed and energy on this particular one, Loretta, who rolled over and pinned him down with one long thigh and opened her blue eyes to survey him.

"What day is it?"

"Friday."

"You going to school?"

He shrugged and extricated himself from under her bone. Lately he'd been staying at Netty's on week nights or whenever he had a girl, but he hadn't meant to sleep with Loretta and not all night at any rate. Such an act seemed too intimate, too husbandly, when all he'd intended was to have her listen to him in the early evening and then have sex.

He watched her sit up and push back her long hair, which was half of her appeal. Netty would kill for such a long, pale mane and in fact had bought one, a synthetic embarrassment in red, which she sometimes wore out at night to Club 21.

LORETTA looked around the small room that was dark last night and thought, as she often did, in spite of herself, "If my parents could see me now." She touched the possibility of this like a hot stone, hoping she was covered by her network of rapidly expanding lies. Last night she was supposed to be staying all night with a friend, Vicki Knapp, in a pink-checked bedroom not much different from her own. Instead she was under the worn sheets of a spare bed that was shoved into a storage room. Out the window, she could see into the lit kitchen of the house next door, where a young woman filled a bottle for her baby from a can of condensed milk. The warmth of this scene entranced Loretta more than anything going on in this room—she could predict it all: Luther's attitude, the coolness of dressing, their lowered eyes.

"We'd better get going," Luther said, half dressed, and annoyed at her dawdling.

He was not entirely sure whether his sister had left yet for her job at Vistron, where she assembled radio components, but he felt her presence through the walls. In fact, she had probably been in this room while they slept (she kept her shoes in there) and this thought—that he and Loretta, tumbled together in sleep, might have been observed by his sister, whose days were spent in a factory and whose nights were spent in a strawberry wig—made him slightly sick.

Loretta stood naked before the window long enough for the

baby in the kitchen below to see a flash of white and look up, but she moved off quickly, picking up her clothes from the dusty floor. She couldn't find her underpants and struggled into her pantyhose without them.

Luther zipped up his pants, annoyed at how many things about her still affected him this morning—the bright patch of hair under her arms, her cushiony ass, the length of her neck as she pulled a sweater over her head and briefly disappeared so that for a moment he was staring at a headless white girl squeezed into pantyhose that looked a size too tight. To quell his desire, he quickly catalogued her faults: she had a cold and had probably given it to him, kissing on him all night; her legs were a little flabby at the thighs—she might become heavy as she got older. He turned away, defeated. He could not see enough faults for this to work right now.

NETTY BIGGS was not authentically surprised by much anymore, but she had been taken aback at seeing her brother and the white girl asleep together that morning when she went into the storage room, not for shoes, as Luther suspected, but simply to see if he was all right. Luther was not always all right now, the way he'd been when he was young. As a kid, he seemed unhurtable: the one who fell down the stairs, head over legs, then stood up like an acrobat and grinned; the one who hadn't cried when their father Horace died on the other side of town last year, in another woman's house, of a heart attack; the one who always figured out what to do when their mother, Annie, ran out of money, and—briefly—imagination. When there was no more bread in the house, no way to pay the electricity bill, Luther was the one who put on his hat and went out into the streets to figure something out, no one ever asked what.

Netty was seven years older than Luther and had helped as

she could, but she was a woman who'd stumbled early by having a child. She knew she had shackled herself, perhaps voluntarily, to diminished possibilities, having seen what would be offered her anyhow. Now she at least had her son, Andre, a strong, blood-filled reason to drive to Vistron each day and move her hands as if by magic. With her son and her job and the tail-end of a desire that she expected to die off shortly, she didn't have much time for Luther, only enough to open a door, to look at him and worry.

But nothing he'd done in the past—the drugs, the suspensions, the knife she once found in his trousers when she did his laundry—had shocked her like the intimacy of the scene she couldn't get out of her mind this morning: the rumpled sheets, the winter light, the arrangement of black and white arms. She had driven the block to her mother's house before she realized it, and decided, late for work or not, she must be meant to go inside.

Annie Biggs was fifty-five years old, but no one could tell this. She looked the way she did now ten years ago and would look the same in another twenty. No one in their family took photographs—or had a camera, for that matter (Andre broke the Polaroid Netty'd received from a boyfriend one Christmas, while taking the camera's first and only photo, a shot of an end table covered with ripped paper and ribbon)—so there would be no way to verify this later. Netty supposed that what had settled on her mother, the early veil of disappointment and petty illness that made her unplaceable, would eventually happen to her. She didn't like to think this, wanted to imagine that she would continue to have the fortitude for Club 21 at least on Saturday nights. But at the same time as Andre grew older, her back had begun to hurt her, and after nights when she couldn't sleep because of furniture payments or a comment from the foreman the previous day, she couldn't bear to look at her reflection in the morning.

She looked like Annie; she loved her mother, but she'd never wanted to look like her.

Annie was in bed now, but she'd been up, Netty could tell by the house smells. She'd made a bacon sandwich and a cup of coffee and washed out some clothes. Then there was the rest of the day. Without a car or money until her next check, she'd gone back under the sheets. Netty hated that Annie did this, yet knew that without the tyranny of Vistron, she'd probably do the same.

"Luther," Annie called out, hopefully, as Netty creaked the stairs.

"No, just me," Netty replied, smiling ruefully. Annie always wished for Luther, her baby, first, and rarely got him.

"I'm just reading the papers," Annie said as Netty came into the room, picking one up from the rumpled covers. Netty knew she had been simply lying there, curled up, awake. "Why aren't you at work?"

"I don't know. I'm going. Just felt like seeing you."

"Something wrong?"

"No, nothing." Netty patted her mother's hand. She sat down beside her and wished they didn't have to lie to each other so much, futile as it was.

"Andre's not sick?"

"Andre's fine." Netty released Annie's hand and said, "Luther stayed over at the house last night."

This was no big deal in itself; Luther stayed everywhere—at Annie's, at his uncle Buddy's; it was hard to pin him down. "With that white girl," she finished.

"Slept *over* with a white girl? Who?"

Netty shrugged. "That blonde he has, Loretta."

"Lord," Annie said, but that was all.

They sat in silence as the bedside clock ticked off the time. It was an old clock from Netty's childhood, and she was surprised that it had lasted this long. Next to it were the vials of ancient remedies that Annie had used all her life, fruitless rubs and balms and emulsions that were labelless; Netty was still not sure where they'd ever come from. They both gazed out the window, only because it was there, in front of them.

IT wasn't until after Annie Biggs had given birth to Netty that she'd realized how much she also wanted a son. But Luther had taken so long in arriving that she'd thought something was wrong, preventing her from bringing another child into the world; that perhaps God had looked down at her crumbling house, her wandering husband, her paltry cupboards and said, "Woman, you've got enough."

That's why she'd cried when the nurse brought long, black, wailing Luther and placed him in her arms. At thirty-seven, she felt his weight as a renewed vote of confidence, from someone. And his birth actually heralded the only good time in her marriage. Horace was forty-six when Luther was born, and it made him feel young again. Annie thought he felt young enough already, if you wanted to look at the evidence, but his unfaithfulness, she knew, was really not proof of much. Horace didn't feel he had anything to prove himself by but his sex, and that wasn't his fault.

In fact, fault, as far as Annie could tell, didn't matter much. She'd thought so once, but then she'd also been young. You had this life and these instincts, and then you loved and suffered, hoped sometimes, in spite of yourself. Although Annie spent much of her day now in bed, she still believed that life was good, all in all. She had a window to look out of and two children, grown and elsewhere, inching their little trails on the world. She liked that—their pathmaking apart from her, troublesome or not. It was the same way she felt about the sun; even in her deepest night, she was pleased it was shining somewhere.

LORETTA eventually rode to school with Luther, but it was a silent drive. They'd both missed homeroom, and the day was ruined, as far as Loretta could tell. She didn't feel normal unless she slept at least ten hours in her own narrow bed, and she hadn't been feeling anything near that lately. She tried fixing herself up in the girls' bathroom and sitting through first period journalism, but it was useless—she could smell Luther's sperm on her, and was sure everyone else could too. She asked for a bathroom pass during reading time and left the building by the back, heading home, she supposed.

At sixteen, she had no place else to go. She had yet to establish a personality that people independently recognized and liked on its own, that caused them to open their doors or invite her inside or yearn for her company. The most she had managed so far was the attention of boys and men, and this she received, without speaking or thinking. Five older men and six younger ones honked or called out to her on her ten-block journey home; she tallied them automatically, like an odometer.

LUTHER left school separately and headed south, in a direction opposite Loretta's. He was a senior this year and knew he would pass because the principal was eager to be rid of him. Luther was not only taller than any of the teachers, but also wore something on his face that only others could see—some reproach, some authority, that kept them from insisting that he do much of anything. He roamed the halls, he smoked, he laughed out loud in the middle of lectures; he wouldn't stand for the pledge of allegiance.

He was already well aware of his facts: that he was a six-foot, two-inch, eighteen-year-old black man, with a strong grip and a large laugh and dim prospects in this small Ohio town with its small Ohio ghetto, a place where he had been born and had already begun to die. But under Loretta's influence, during the time they'd been together, he'd begun to imagine a future of vague glory, where, without much effort, he'd right things, turn the world around. After they made love, he'd occasionally talk about these things with her, not only because she seemed the type who'd want to hear them, but because the simple act of their lying together still felt almost revolutionary to him.

"You'll do something, I know you will," Loretta would say afterwards, lying in the drafty rooms of their spent love, and Luther'd try to forget that she'd been dozing throughout most of his talk, that even as he was speaking, she had the full intention of leaving him shortly, of driving home in her father's Buick, equipped with climate control and full of premium gas, to a house so soundly designed, so carefully decorated, that no one, neither she nor he, believed that the life in it, nor what it signified, would ever fall or crumble.

ANNIE was in her second or third stage of dreaming by eleven that morning when Luther came by for his daily visit. Her dreams started out bad but got better as the day wore on. Usually someone dead would appear in the early ones—Tiffany or Horace or her father—and she would just become accustomed to their being alive again, of their deaths as mistaken nightmares, when she would wake herself up. But her later dreams were pleasant and centered on her early life; she was always slim and pretty—her true self, she thought—in these dreams, and there were often flowers, usually pink roses, on tables, in bowls. Her dreaming life was complicated and occupied much of her time; she slept, not so much because she was tired, but because she liked what she eventually saw.

Just before Luther's steps woke her, Annie dreamed of a white cat, a stray, who had ended up in the house. Annie and Luther both disliked cats, were nervous of their sly faces and claws, but this one was so grateful for its milk, so graceful when it rubbed against her ankles, that Annie let it stay on her rug. In the dream, Luther walked in and railed at her for feeding it, but when the cat lifted its face to him, he stopped. Stopped, just as he'd stopped now, in reality, at the foot of her bed.

"I'm all right," she said, instantly awake and knowing that he sometimes came upon her like this and feared she wasn't breathing. He seemed so frightened of this that she thought it might be the way he was going to find her eventually. That was good from one point of view—she'd gladly die here in her old fragrant bed and be discovered by her son—but disturbing in the sense that she would cause him grief, something she had tried never to do.

"No school today?" she asked when he didn't say anything. Luther broke his position when she smiled. He had another reprieve; she was still alive.

"I had some business to take care of," he answered, sitting, knowing she wouldn't ask more.

Annie pulled herself up flush with the headboard and surveyed the change in his face. It was different every time she saw him; she didn't regret that she was no longer young, but was sorry that he still had to be.

"You need anything from the store?"

"Juice," Annie answered. "Maybe some vegetables."

"What kind?"

"You pick. You'll be the one eating them."

Luther looked out the window; he'd have to stay around and help her more. He had so many good intentions as far as Annie was concerned, but he always seemed to run out of time.

"I'm gonna be staying here more now," he said, as if this would make him do it.

"Netty don't mind you over there. Course, I miss you."

Luther looked at her sharply. "You talk to Netty lately?"

"This morning."

Luther continued to look at her, but she only smiled and handed him her dream book. "I don't have my glasses. Look up cat in there and read what it says."

Luther turned the pages—cane, car, cat. "A young female of the species," he read out, not looking at her. "You dreamed about a cat?"

She nodded. "A white one."

He handed back the book, his part done. "So what do you want me to do?"

"Get some money out of my pocketbook and play on it," she said.

WHEN Elaine Johnson's father, Junior, dropped her off at school that morning, he pulled up at the intersection where Luther and Loretta were crossing—Luther walking slightly ahead, as if to distance himself from Loretta, who was plucking her way through slush in her skimpy shoes.

"Look at that," Junior said derisively, but Elaine gathered her books and pretended not to see. She did not want to be bothered by the same things as her father, one of the most staid and conservative men in town. He owned Johnson's Funeral Home and spent all day working there, doing what Elaine did not like to imagine, then came home at night with a formaldehyde smell and broad, strong opinions about the blacks who lived around them. He was as light-skinned as Elaine, and she'd heard rumors all her life that he'd passed as white in the navy.

"I guess there's not enough sisters out there for these young punks," Junior muttered as Elaine opened the car door and slipped out, thinking that her father was hard to figure out, and that she was glad she'd soon be free of him. She had one more year of high school, one more year of his criticizing her wardrobe, her posture, her boyfriends. No one pleased him, or ever would.

It was just a month since she'd been selected Union's first black homecoming queen. Before then, she'd only been viewed as light-skinned and bright, but her value had gone up considerably after she'd been driven around the football field wearing a tiara in a Chevy Camaro with her date.

Nobody black in town had ever been chosen like this before, and Elaine had underestimated the impact it would have on her life. Back in the neighborhood, old women took her hand and gazed up at her as if she had won something grander than a local beauty contest; children stopped kicking their balls, reverentially, when she walked by. But it was the black men who'd changed most. Except for her father.

"I'll pick you up at four," he called out the window as she moved off.

"That's all right. I'll walk."

"You heard me. Four."

She looked at him with brief hatred as he put his big car in gear and rolled down the hill, as if in a yacht. As Elaine approached the school she saw Luther Biggs at the window of the second floor stairwell, studying her as he headed up.

TWO was Annie's lucky number, she'd forgotten why, and she won $222.21 on the number Luther played for her, the best she'd done all year. He gave it to her in an old envelope that weekend when he stopped by.

"Not bad," he said as she took it, counted it, then handed most of it back to him.

"Why don't you go over to Clyde Ewans and buy a ham or something. I feel like cooking tonight."

"I was gonna bring someone by."

"Good," she said, getting out of bed. "I'll cook for them, too."

"For Loretta."

"For Loretta then," Annie replied, smiling at him. He'd just had a haircut; his scalp was oiled and she wanted to kiss its dampness. Any disappointment this boy brought her was first filtered through the net of her love for him. What could he ever do that would totally displease her? Only kill someone, she decided.

"Get me a pork roast then," she said as he headed out. "And some yams, big ones."

LORETTA was dressing for a slumber party at Vicki Knapp's. Her lies were becoming sloppy: juniors at Senior High rarely had slumber parties anymore, and in any case would never be dressing for one so carefully, but she was wearing her other excuses thin. Her mother, her primary warden, did not seem any more suspicious than usual, although it was hard to tell with her anymore. She'd begun working full time, key-punching fertilizer data into a computer, and returned home with bleary eyes and a drunken look. She could barely organize dinner, let alone sniff out Loretta's lies, at least so Loretta hoped.

Still, her mother kept track of Loretta in other subtle ways. She was the only one who knew when Loretta's last tetanus shot was, and her exact bra size; she even knew the dates of her periods, which she marked on the gas station calendar in the kitchen—a red star for Loretta, a black check for her. Loretta noticed that they had their periods in the same week of the month, occasionally on the same day. This meant that Loretta's father was often subjected to a double dose of irritability, but he never complained.

Loretta had not asked Luther where they were going when he had called and hung up and then called again, his signal to her. She thought they would probably drive around and then go make love, since that was their pattern now. Loretta thought this was as good a date as she'd had in the past with white boys. They wanted the same thing, even if they bought you a cheeseburger beforehand, but she could not stand their inexperienced small talk, their drawn-out approach, the blush on their pale necks. Luther led her into the dark and knew what to do with her, without stumblings or apologies. His remoteness made him desirable, as if he had large, manly things on his mind, which sometimes bubbled up and out of him, especially when she held him in her arms. She'd always been drawn to the elegance of blacks and thought that they must have been subjugated, like women, because they were so clearly superior. She did not know why or how she had come to think these things, but she thought them anyway, and didn't mind throwing away whatever reputation she had by being with Luther. Already she'd found a note taped on her locker that said "Nigger Lover," and there would probably be worse in the future. But for now she was more concerned with adequately covering up a pimple on her chin, the hard, painful kind she got this time of the month.

NETTY BIGGS found the white girl's underpants when she made up the spare bed on Saturday. She also found a hairpin, a hooped earring, and a black tuft of pubic hair in the sheets, but these were from other girls Luther'd brought in the past, and she knew the underwear was from Loretta. They were bikinis of pink tricot, with lace around the legs and "Sunday" sewn in contrasting red thread. Netty'd never been able to wear this style because of her thighs, but she remembered the age when she had wanted to, when she had coveted all the kinds of things the white girl had strewn around her room—the rabbit jacket, the small strapped shoes, the charm bracelet that hung limply from her wrist in sleep.

Most of this impossible yearning had left her after Andre, although she still could not help coveting that hair. As she took off the sheets, she found a single strand under the pillow; when she held it up to the light, she saw that the ends were split, like a fork.

After all the trouble she'd had with whites, it was hard to accept them sleeping in her house. In her house, which she could

barely afford because the management of Vistron refused to recognize the seniority of blacks. Under her sheets, which she hardly
had time to wash because of the overtime she worked in order to
meet the mortgage. In the storage room next to her son, who'd
started to ask irksome questions lately that she didn't feel like
answering.

As she cleaned the room, she tried to work up an anger at
Luther, then at the girl, but it wouldn't sustain itself. She'd been
led into other women's rooms by men herself, and all she ended
up holding onto was the remembrance of waking up, no longer
young, in someone else's bed.

LUTHER put a piece of pork into his mouth that evening, then
a spoonful of apple sauce, and tried to let the pleasurable combination of tastes console him. Annie said he was always putting
things in his mouth when he was little; that he ate dirt, ice,
paint, whatever he could get his hands on. His tastes were more
sophisticated now, and often a number of flavors were required
before he was satisfied.

But nothing worked tonight. He didn't know why he was here,
at his mother's, with Loretta, who had already stumbled over the
entryway, spilled a glass of juice, and just now whispered to him
that she couldn't eat much because she was getting diarrhea.

"You want to lay down?" he asked, unused to anyone, especially a woman, confiding to him about how she felt.

"No, I want to keep trying. Everything looks so good," she
insisted, her face overbright.

The pork roast looked so good to her, in fact, that she was
tempted to pull off the whole expanse of crackling skin. But mostly
she wanted to keep trying because she had seen, all at once, as
she'd entered this house and smelled lemon oil and meat and
something vaguely like mothballs, that this round, kind-faced
woman who wore a black wool dress and Luther's eyes and nose

as if they were accessories, had gone to a lot of trouble for her.

She had never been anywhere so—warm. Everything about the two rooms she passed through and the woman who led her through them made her feel at home; she wanted to sink down in the overstuffed couch, put her hands in front of the red smile of the electric fire, poke her face into the pot moaning fragrantly on the stove. She wanted to do all these things at once, and the surprise of this feeling and place after what she had expected made some large organ inside her contract.

Annie, who had spent the last two hours noticing anew everything that was wrong with her house, could not keep from smiling. Even though Netty had described Loretta to her, she had not expected this—this shy, faintly pretty, bumbling girl who looked as if she wasn't even finished yet. She'd smiled right off, as soon as she opened the door and Luther said, "Momma, Loretta," and the girl had blinked those new eyes and put out her pink paw and almost tripped into her arms.

And when Annie had said, "I hope you like pork roast" as she led the way to the kitchen, Loretta had replied, "Oh, I like anything," and followed like a puppy, leaving Luther still kicking the snow off his boots in the hall.

In the last half hour, under Annie's questioning, Luther had learned more about Loretta than he'd gleaned from being with her over a month—where her father and mother worked, where her grandparents lived, that she even had grandparents, that lavender was her favorite color. He was not accustomed to being ignored at his own mother's table and wondered if he really needed or even wanted to know all this. He looked up at Annie as she was telling Loretta about a blue Ford an uncle of hers once had and couldn't believe the light in his mother's face, her charm. And Loretta looked as if someone had plugged her in; she'd bitten off her lipstick, so that her mouth was pale as she spooned in kale, evidently forgetting her diarrhea.

"Baby, have some more," Annie said to Luther suddenly. She

and Loretta had stopped their talk and were looking at him in a measured silence, as if remembering that he was the reason they were together.

"I'm full," he said, rising and walking to the stereo, pretending to be absorbed in picking out some music.

"IS she really sick?" Annie asked him later when Loretta went upstairs to the bathroom.

"Just nervous, I guess."

"She didn't know you all were coming here?"

"No," he admitted, amazed again at his own folly. Even if he never saw Loretta again, Annie would be sure to bring her up, and Loretta would never again be satisfied with a quick tumble somewhere nameless in the dark. He'd shown her where he was from and she had sat in it; he couldn't believe how intimate this felt.

When he finally went upstairs to see how she was, he found her sitting on the toilet, studying the back of a jar of hair grease.

"Sorry it stinks," she said, like a sister, when he walked in and pulled a face. She held up the jar. "Do you use this?"

"No," he said tersely. "You about ready to go?"

She saw his expression and pulled a length of toilet paper from the roll as a spasm of gas and liquid filled the bowl; Luther backed out and shut the door.

LORETTA did not want to leave the tiny bathroom, with its clanking pipes and rusted sink; she didn't want to go home. There, everything was new and bright—Avon decanters in novelty shapes and everywhere the pervasive smell of Lysol. This was as a bathroom should be.

Inside the hair-grease jar Loretta found the imprint of many fingers, or the same fingers many times, and a few loose black hairs. After she flushed the toilet, she stood in front of the mirror and spread the grease on a strand of hair. The wave went out of it; the strand hung straight and lank.

WAITING in the car while Annie gave Loretta some meat to take home, Luther thought of Elaine Johnson, probably because her cousin Louis had just driven by. She had sprung up in his mind during the last few months like something forgotten, then remembered again. Her appeal had always been masked by the fact that she was not only acceptable but smart. She didn't smoke or drink or fuck, as far as he knew, and he only saw her with her studious boyfriend, Tyrone, a chemistry whiz, as they walked by the house, burdened, absurdly it seemed to him, with books. Seeing the two of them, so serious, made Luther mad. It almost made him lean out the window and yell at them, "You fools might as well come get high as study. This is Union!"

Of course he didn't do this, and made sure that they never saw him watching at all. He wasn't getting high lately himself; he felt that he needed all his wits about him, that shortly he was going to have to figure out something complicated.

And this is what it was, he thought now, as Annie turned on the porch light and stood directly behind Loretta, who threw a small shadow across her girth. He watched those little shoes—pink, they were, pink in the winter!—move down to him, saw his mother's hand move back and forth in a wave, interrupting the light.

ANNIE couldn't remember if she'd ever told that Uncle Harry story before or whether no one had ever listened to it as seriously as Loretta. It was a silly story really:

My uncle Harry saved from his foundry job for three years to get a certain baby-blue Ford. He didn't even take time off to marry, he was so busy saving—that car was his whole life. He finally got it when he was thirty-six years old, and that same year, that same month even, he had it stolen right out from under him when he parked it in front of Wright's Pool Hall. He was so upset about this—he didn't even have insurance yet—that he took to bed and almost lost his job. His mother Nervine was alive then—Nervie, we called her, for short. She'd been widowed for so long and Harry had worked so much that she didn't know what to do with a man underfoot. So she called her brother's sons who lived across town and asked if one of them'd come over and try to cheer Harry up. Willy, the youngest, said he had something that would do the trick—a spin in his new car. And sure enough, Willy pulled up in Harry's blue car, except it had been painted red by then, but Harry swore he knew it was his, knew the steering wheel even; he had that car memorized. He was still strong enough to get right out of his bed and pull Willie from the car and fight him in the snow. And while they were rolling around, that Ford just slipped out of gear and rolled down the hill and smacked into a brick wall.

Annie didn't realize until she was in the middle of this tale how much she liked to talk. Later, she worried that she had told it to a white girl at all: it made blacks look like thieving fools; it would make Loretta think—she didn't know what. But the flattery of someone's attention!—it was even better than words of love. She had married Horace for much less, for a few weeks of his walking in her direction, unbuttoning her, smiling once or twice—for as little as that. He'd died never knowing her middle name or her exact birthdate (he only knew it was in the teens, in the autumn), and what perhaps was worse, she'd never told him. But who liked to tell something that wasn't heard? That would be as sad as the canary she'd had when she was a girl, who down in the basement, covered with a black rag, sang into the night. No, even sadder, for a bird song was beautiful no matter who heard it, like a never-looked-upon flower. Annie realized all at once that she had quit singing—or blooming—years ago, almost as soon as she'd started.

WHEN Netty stopped over at her mother's Monday morning, she was shocked to find Annie moving the furniture around. Annie used her hips and pelvis to push things, and Netty had always thought, probably unmedically, that it was all this undue strain that had caused her to require a hysterectomy.

"What are you doing? Wait a minute!" Netty said as soon as she walked in, but Annie had just thrust the couch into the corner.

"I got sick of looking at it where it was," Annie said, her face flushed, then headed toward the kitchen, as Netty, noting changes all around her, followed. Dusty doilies were gone, and knick-nacks that had stood in the same place for twenty-five years had been rearranged. A porcelain dancer holding a pink skirt whose glass pleats had fascinated Netty as a child had been washed and was now facing a chipped Santa she didn't even recognize. What was going on here?

Annie pressed her thighs against the warm oven as Netty sat down. At least this was normal, a relief. Annie often stood like this, pressed into the warmth, even when the stove was empty. But now she bent to pull out a tin of cornbread, which she brought to the table. She sat down across from Netty, saying, "Don't worry. I just woke up feeling good. Guess it takes a minute to get used to."

"I'm glad you feel good," Netty said, still suspicious. Something in this house, which she felt was still partly hers, had changed since her last visit. She took the block of cornbread that Annie gave her and began picking at it, trying to remember why she'd come. She felt as if she'd had something to bring her mother, but realized she had nothing in her hands.

She heard a bump upstairs and then Luther's step coming down.

They were silent as he hesitated in the living room, then continued on to the kitchen. He didn't look happy to see either one of them.

"Who moved that couch?" he shot off at his mother. "You?"

When she nodded, he turned his back to them and frowned. "I don't want you changing things around, hear? Just leave everything like it was."

Annie stood up, got a cup of coffee, and handed it to him. "Luther, sit down. You sound just like your daddy and I don't feel like thinking about him now."

Luther looked over at Netty, as if for help, but she only raised an eyebrow. She hadn't seen him since the night he'd stayed at her house and began to see that all of this upheaval was connected with Loretta somehow.

Luther took the coffee and went into the living room where they heard him sit on the couch.

"Well, I was feeling good," Annie said ruefully. "You want to help me move this refrigerator out? I can't get behind it to clean."

Netty was late to Vistron for the second time that month because after the refrigerator, Annie wanted to move the stove; then she wanted Netty to climb a ladder to change some lightbulbs. It had been so long since her mother had asked her to do something concrete that Netty couldn't refuse. She felt a desire to stake some renewed claim to this house, which with its dust and sameness was the one steadfast port in her life, and she rearranged a coffee table and moved a lamp without Annie's even requesting it.

THAT week, Luther failed a geometry test by turning in a blank test sheet, initiated sex with Adremma Butler, who had his friend Langdon's child, and started a fight in a back hall with a freshman, who he insisted later, in the guidance office, had called him nigger.

He avoided Loretta, Annie, and Netty, and stayed in the chaotic jumble of his Uncle Buddy's house. Buddy had been an air-
plane mechanic during the war and now was a spot welder and a
drunk. Or so said Annie, who Luther thought was prejudiced,
since Buddy was the twin of Luther's father, Horace.

Luther sometimes felt that Buddy, such as he was, was the
only father he had. He'd always liked the vague approval, the
envy even, that Buddy bestowed on him whenever he brought a
girl around, or a joint, or especially a six-pack of beer.

Buddy managed to rise from his stupor often enough to entan-
gle himself with women, never very satisfactorily, if what Luther
witnessed was any sign. And he'd been doing this for so many
years that most nights when Luther stayed with him, some woman
or other would show up, her heels clicking up his driveway,
wanting something from Buddy—something he had hinted at, or
promised or given only partially. Buddy had a lifetime of tactics
for soothing and stalling, and Luther usually nursed a beer and
listened with appreciation as his old uncle cajoled and lied through
his screendoor.

"Crazy bitch," he'd exclaim when he came back into the living room, making Luther laugh. But that was before Luther had
woken up, morning after morning, in the gray jumble of Buddy's
house, where there was never any juice in the refrigerator or
bread in the breadbox. In the morning Luther noted his uncle's
chronic cough and his knotted hair and his flat daytime eyes.
This is what happens to men without women, Luther thought
on the fourth day as he watched Buddy sip beer for breakfast,
and on Thursday he went back to his mother.

OF all the things that annoyed Elaine Johnson about Tyrone
Davis, tonight it was his teeth. They were white as a dog's, and
he showed a lot of them as he sat around her family's dining room

table. Her mother, Helene, had insisted that they celebrate the fact that both of them were on the honor role the second straight year in a row. Junior went along with it, although Elaine was sure that he wouldn't have if he could have thought of a legitimate reason.

Tyrone was as agreeable as Junior was not. After an hour of listening to her father playing the devil's advocate on every possible position with Tyrone cheerfully fielding him, Elaine decided that they liked this kind of sparring and that her stomach had been knotted all through dinner in vain.

"You didn't eat much, Elaine," Helene said during a lull.

"I'm not very hungry."

"That's a first." Tyrone smiled in a way so knowing that it made Junior angry.

"I've seen plenty of nights when Elaine hasn't finished a meal," Junior said as his wife cleared the table. " 'Course that'll change once she's out in the world and sees what it costs to live."

Speculation on the kind of life Elaine would have later was common here; they all had an idea. Junior saw a scholarship, a legal degree, and great gratitude for the early leadership he'd provided. He half saw a husband, but couldn't fashion one that suited him, so he left that part blank. Helene saw her daughter with someone like Tyrone, though probably not Tyrone personally, then a teaching or nursing degree and a child later, preferably a girl or two.

Tyrone saw himself and Elaine vividly together in a student apartment, where he would be studying something exceedingly more difficult. Elaine's schedule would be light enough that she'd have time to bake for him in the evening and listen to him in the morning, possibly before she went to work. He knew she was bright, but it seemed a weak and general intelligence compared to his, so he was unsure where she should put it. Of course, if he became an engineer, as he planned, she wouldn't have to place it anywhere. Except on him; he wanted Elaine, especially her long body, which she had yet to let him experience, in the same way he coveted fine cars.

"Time enough for that," he thought as he looked at her, content with his full stomach in this moderate, well-kept house, ignoring the answering stare of Junior, who was, in Tyrone's mind, only a mortician, an aging father, who'd already had his chance.

THE night Luther came back from Buddy's, Annie washed his hair, something he hadn't let her do since he was a boy. As far as she could tell, he presented the back of his neck to her, that long curve, the most vulnerable spot of the body, and she couldn't resist. He wouldn't have jammed himself into the kitchen sink, clanging pots, had he not at least expected her to try. After she was done soaping his hair, she rubbed the knot in his neck with one warm and sudsy hand. She tried to block out the room they were in and all their worries and, through her hands, give him everything she had.

When she was done, he wrapped his head in a towel, lit a cigarette, and sat down in front of the TV.

"You're not staying in tonight, are you?" she asked him.

"Why? You don't want me to?"

"Just never saw you stay put so early before."

Luther's gaze wandered from the television. All the while he'd been at Buddy's, he'd worried about how the house would look after he'd been gone, about how his mother would act; he'd even worried that Loretta had called. But he was relieved now, with his damp head and soothed neck, to see that things were pretty much the same as when he'd left. Of course, the couch was on the other side of the room, but he was almost used to that.

"You really liked her," he said during a commercial, and Annie walked over and turned the set down.

"I like most people," she replied evenly. "Now why don't you tell me what's wrong."

"I don't think I should bring her over again. I didn't think I should see her even."

Annie looked at the TV as the program came back on. A white man appeared on the screen with a gun and shot it, twice, at someone.

"Then don't," she said finally. "Since when have I got anything to say about who you see or not?"

"C'mon, momma," Luther said, turning off the TV and ripping the towel from his head.

"C'mon, what? You bring a girl here and I feed and talk to her and then you bluster around and go off to Buddy's all week. Go on and love who you want, Luther. I've never meddled in that—" She stopped, and he looked at her.

"But what?"

"But don't hurt her. Don't hurt nobody," she went on, almost regretfully. "I shouldn't even ask you that, but I am."

She went into the kitchen, although Luther knew she was already done. It hurt him to see her so flustered.

"Who said anything about hurting anybody?" he called to her, but Annie turned on the water and pretended not to hear him.

LORETTA'S health teacher, Mrs. Sims, gave a lecture on condoms to her all-girl class that Friday.

"And remember, *you* have to make the guy use it, because he won't ever want to stop and put one on."

This was a brash lecture for Senior High, but Mrs. Sims was young and modern and newly married and didn't yet realize how far she could go. Months later she would be ratted on by several of her less than virginal students, including Vicki Knapp, who was covered now in a wash of pink, even though she'd had oral sex with her new boyfriend only the night before.

"God, do you believe she said all that?" Vicki whispered as she and Loretta were walking down the hall after class.

The lecture had come too late for Loretta, who had just missed her period, but she felt she had to defend Mrs. Sims's unorthodox courage, which she sometimes hoped she was exhibiting herself.

"There probably aren't two virgins left in that class. Why shouldn't she talk about it?"

Vicki didn't reply, her gaze trained down the hall as it always was, looking out for who was going to be noticing her next. There were only girls and freshman boys flooding toward them, so she briefly gave Loretta her attention.

"I wasn't going to tell you this, but you better be more careful. Rex said that one of the guys saw you in Luther's car after the last home game, and Hank Black . . ."

"Hank Black told everyone he fingered me when all I did was eat french fries with him at the Big Boy. I despise Hank Black."

"Yeah, well, I know he's an asshole, but still, you know how the guys are."

A clot of senior boys was suddenly bearing down on them, and Vicki positioned her breasts under her mohair and was lost. Loretta averted her gaze as one of them plucked Vicki aside and spoke to her in low tones. Loretta moved on, thinking that all of this was probably for nothing anyway, since Luther hadn't called her in nearly a week. But then she thought of Annie, and that bathroom, and the long cooking smell of pork roast, and she managed to hold up her head briefly as she approached algebra, her final class. Held it up long enough for Luther to see her from a distance, alone and sad-mouthed, and after that he gave up resisting her.

II

ANNIE told no one in the following weeks when she dreamed she had another baby; a girl it was, round and nut-colored, with indescribable eyes. Such dreams, along with Loretta's visits, kept her excited most of the time. She baked cakes and she remembered things from her earliest years of childhood, and all of them—the floral print of an aunt's apron, the smell of a peony in sunshine—opened further into the intricate, half-forgotten tales of her life. She had to keep herself from asking Luther exactly when he was bringing Loretta by, because it was only then that it all came together in a way she found satisfying.

Seated at her kitchen table in the warm room while Luther shoveled snow outside, Loretta would eat one square of yellow cake after another while Annie talked on. Loretta kept such track of what Annie told her that she even tried to tie it together sometimes.

"So was that the same Sonny who went blind and your mother took care of before she died?" she'd ask, and Annie would nod happily, realizing that the underarms of her housedress were drenched with sweat.

Luther had learned to stay in the living room when he came in from outside until Annie was done. From where he sat, he couldn't hear his mother's exact words, only their comforting hum. He could see the side of Loretta's head, touched by window light, and smell whatever had been baked mingle with the pot of coffee that perked on low throughout the day.

With the snow outside and this warmth inside, Luther allowed himself the embarrassment of being happy with only this—two women in another room who would both turn their heads in affection if he should stand up now and fill the doorway.

But he waited until there was a lull in the flow, and Annie said, "Well . . ." before he got up and went in and ate himself.

He was always amused when Loretta ate again, with him.

"You're getting fat, girl," he said one day, patting her stomach, and Annie, watching them, had to turn away at the sudden
end she saw.

LORETTA never actually told Luther in words that she was having a baby; she had discussions with Annie over the calendar in
the kitchen, conversations he was on the periphery of as he pretended to listen to music or read. She went upstairs on several
occasions to take hot baths with powders in the water. He saw
her take tablets that came from dusty vials that had sat at the
back of kitchen cabinets for years. He noted her face, pinched
and wan, after she'd brayed into the bathroom like a donkey.
But neither she nor his mother included him in their circle of
awareness, knowing instinctively the truth: that he would know
neither what to do or to say.

It was a bad time all round: Buddy had lost his job spot welding over at Union Electric; Netty had discovered her boyfriend
was already married to someone else; for the first time Luther lost
a good deal of weight. Everybody seemed to be losing except for
Loretta, who was discernibly fuller each time he saw her; she
even gained weight around her neck. But it was not until the
third month of her pregnancy that they actually talked about it.
They were getting dressed after making love behind the shower
curtain that was the door to his room; Luther didn't really feel
like doing it anymore, but thought, mistakenly, that she did.
She was turned away from him, pulling on a Playtex girdle that
looked as if it had been designed for a child.

"Wearing that thing can't be any good," he said, watching her
struggle.

"Any good for who?"

"For the baby."

She showed him a mean, vexed face as she snapped the elastic around her. "Well, if it's not good for the baby, it's probably not good for me either."

"Loretta," he said, starting toward her, but she suddenly raised her hands to her face and, standing there in her girdle and boots, started to cry.

Luther had never seen her cry before and found the sight of it shocking. She's just a kid herself, he thought, as he put his arms around her, the observation of an older voice that occasionally roamed about his head.

"I can't keep it. They're sending me away," Loretta blubbered into the collar of a knit sweater he had just picked up from the dry cleaners, and in that moment, standing behind the ripped shower curtain in his room with a white girl drooling on him, Luther felt for the first time the realness of their situation. He saw he'd never hold this child; the only contact he'd have was now, in its blind, embryonic existence. Feeling this strongly, he led Loretta back to the bed and carefully laid her down; then with difficulty he worked off the girdle and rubbed the white round globe of her stomach.

"I don't want that girdle for either one of you," he said.

THREE and a half months after that afternoon, Netty Biggs met Elaine Johnson with a tight little smile. She'd seen photos of her, wearing a crown, in the paper several months back, and now here she was, mussed and wary, emerging from her storage room. She wished Luther would give her some warning when he switched girls like this. She'd just become as used to having Loretta around as she ever would be, and now here was someone else.

Netty had learned about Loretta's pregnancy weeks before when she'd walked into her mother's house and found Annie peering into Loretta's eyes with a flashlight.

"Knocked up," Annie'd announced by way of greeting, and Loretta had spread her hand like a starfish on top of a calendar on the table, over the waning days of March.

Had Loretta asked, Netty would have told her that she remembered how it felt, those weeks between when the blood stopped and the nausea started, when your body tricked your brain into believing that nothing had changed. Tricked it so long that it grew too late to sit in a hot bath or lift a bed or take quinine until your ears rang, because maybe you didn't want to do anything about it anyhow.

Netty knew a baby would change a white girl's life in a way it could have never changed hers, and she surprised herself by thinking that if Loretta asked her opinion, she'd tell her to give it up, and leave her path clear for the future. She'd waited for Loretta to talk to her and in the end was grateful that she hadn't. Annie would have never forgiven such advice, let alone Luther, and in the long run, Netty perhaps could not have forgiven herself.

So she was glad when Loretta'd asked instead about her pie-crusts and mascara, when she'd stood behind as Netty fried. Netty had even taught her to knit so she would have something to do with those skittish white hands. Loretta had insisted that she was going to make Luther a sweater, but when Netty had given her an old ball of black acrylic to practice with, she'd just kept on knitting the same twenty stitches until there was a long, narrow trail over her lap. Netty had taken a perverse pleasure in with-holding further lessons about purling and casting off. Until she was ready to tell her, Loretta had been stuck doing only what she'd been taught. But since Loretta had been sent away to a home for unwed mothers, Netty felt a little ashamed of herself.

And now here was another one, more familiar, less trouble. Netty wasn't particularly impressed by the homecoming queen business, although she knew Luther would be swayed by such glamour. He'd let his hair grow out from the short cut he'd worn since he was a boy—an afro, he called it. Everyone in the last issue of *Jet* was wearing one, even Lou Rawls. Elaine's hair was still processed in a pageboy.

A mussed pageboy now, as she smiled weakly at Netty. But no matter how light-skinned or popular Elaine was, Netty knew her, at least enough to be comfortable when Luther left them alone to warm up his car.

"Luther wants us to get married right away, so I guess we'll be family," Elaine said in a strangely flat tone.

"Oh, girl," Netty thought, but said instead, with a shrug, "I guess we probably are anyhow."

A WEEK later, Elaine Johnson married Luther Biggs in the county courthouse in Cincinnati. No one in her family ever forgave her for not having a proper wedding; they forgot she hadn't occasionally, but somehow they never forgave it. As the first black homecoming queen, she was expected to be a role model. She was supposed to have her train and veil described in the *Herald News*, to let her parents rent the Elks and serve up a catered ham. She was supposed to let them wheel her grandmother in from her old folk's home in Marion so that she could blink and smile in confusion, recognizing no one. Her mother Helene said all this over the phone, after the fact, to Elaine, who was calling from a phone booth on Route 75 while Luther got gas.

Elaine hadn't even asked why Luther wanted to go all the way to Cincinnati. The analytical part of her brain, the part she'd used to solve geometry, had shut down sometime soon after she and Luther'd made love in his sister's house.

After that sex, the first for her, which had lasted all one Saturday afternoon and night, she felt as if something had been knocked down in her, like a power line. She could barely gather together who she was. But there was an interim period, a short one, when her faculties were still flickering and she saw that something about this was wrong; that you didn't make love with an essential stranger, then seriously consider his proposal of marriage in less than twenty-four hours. She knew this wasn't what you did, but she was doing it anyhow. In no time, her body, long neglected, had grown large and brave and was thinking for the rest of her. It ignored how melancholy Luther seemed, even as they made love; it ignored how he pushed this fast elopement, placing hands on her breasts when she protested, turning new and dangerous knobs.

It had to be done now, in the heat of it, he insisted, and the why curled up inside her like a dog. He would take care of everything, he promised as they lay in bed, although even as he talked he seemed too weak to rise up.

But he had risen and drawn her with him, until here she was on the side of the road, with a ring on her hand and her last name gone, hanging up on her mother for the first time in her life.

LATER that night, Luther and Elaine sat in front of Annie's house with Elaine's possessions piled in the back of the car.

As he came out of his fever, the odometer told Luther that he'd driven a round trip of three hundred thirty-one miles; his pockets said that he'd spent the $250 he'd managed to save last year; and the young woman beside him wore a zircon that was a clear indication of his marriage. He already regretted his rashness. Now there would be another set of eyes in his front seat surveying his path, another pair of feet braced on his rubber mats if he drove too fast. There would be no more escapes to Buddy's, to Netty's. He couldn't even think about Loretta.

He got out of the car and opened the trunk, so that it rained on Elaine's wool skirts, her raccoon collared coat, the silk pumps she'd worn as queen.

"C'mon in," he mouthed through the car window as he grabbed a pile and started up the steps.

The house was dark except for the living room and Elaine felt more at home in the Buick. But when another light went on upstairs, she sighed and turned off the car.

"It's my life," she'd proclaimed earlier as she'd pulled a suitcase full of sweaters and shoes out of her parents' house. It had been impossible to pack her vast, promising past—she would have needed crates and time and help. Luther'd remained smoking in the car.

"It's yours all right. So throw it away," Junior had yelled. "Go live on Sugar Street and work at Woolworth's and get knocked up just like everybody else."

Part of what Elaine had hoped to escape was expectations, but she saw now that she'd only traded one set for another. Brides didn't sulk in the rain on their wedding nights, at least she didn't think so. As she got out, Elaine saw that Luther had dropped one of her satin nightgowns on the side of the street in a puddle. It was so perfect, so what Junior would have expected, that she laughed out loud.

NETTY bought herself a new living room suite at Rink's Bargain City after Annie dreamed about one. Lately dreams were the only thing Netty could get her mother to talk about.

"And then it turned out that Daddy'd had another wife all along and we'd just never known about it," Annie finished one morning when Netty stopped by.

Netty nodded. It was hard to remain interested in anyone else's dreams, and her mind was wandering. She could hear Elaine leafing through a magazine in Luther's room down the hall. What was going on in this house that all the women were in bed? Netty hated to ask why Elaine wasn't in school, finishing up the year. Netty'd only stopped because they wanted her to go to adult classes at night—otherwise she would have continued forever. She loved the morning bustle with her books, sitting in class, expecting something.

"Why do you think you're dreaming about him all of a sudden?" she asked finally, realizing she may have slighted her mother.

"Loretta should be due around September," Annie answered instead.

"September," Netty repeated, but she couldn't keep her mind on Loretta, although her mother seemed to have no problem. She was thinking about her new beige tweed living-room set and the cigarette hole her latest boyfriend, Melvin, had burned in the couch the other night. She thought of him as her last indulgence, her final man; she was sure that when he left she'd never have the energy for another one.

The door slammed, and heavy steps climbed the stairs.

"Luther?" Annie called and sat up straighter as he entered the room, his eyes bleary, from reefer or drink, Netty couldn't tell. The other day he'd told her he was thinking of opening a beauty salon, financed she couldn't imagine how.

"Hey, mama," he said, kissing them both soundly and unbuttoning a new suede jacket. Then the bed springs squeaked down the hall, and he backed out again, as Netty watched him, wondering what would become of him, what would become of them all.

EVERYBODY expected Elaine to get pregnant, so she did in the first weeks of her marriage, seeing that she might as well. She'd go back to adult classes after the baby. Unlike Netty she didn't care about all that now.

So this was it, she thought, sitting in Luther's boy's room, looking out at a brick wall. She wasn't surprised that she only appreciated what she'd had now that she'd lost it; it was possibly the only way she would have appreciated it, ever. She thought of the leather-bound Brittanicas in Junior's den. It was through them that she'd learned the strange facts that now swam through her mind in this new inertia. She thought of the exports of Brazil, the moons of Jupiter, the chemical composition of salt. For what reason had she ever learned all this, she and Tyrone, huddled like eunuchs over equations night after night? And she missed her mother's garden and their backyard where geese flew overhead in perfect symmetry at twilight. There was only a muddy alley behind Annie's house, and geese only seemed to fly over when you had a yard.

She dreamed often of homecoming night, which she began to view as the high point of her life. She was glad she had it to dream about, otherwise what would have occupied her nights? Not pleasant dreams, but the old nightmares: Junior simply walking into a room for one of his lectures—that had been nightmare enough. Watching a term paper she'd spent hours typing blow out an open window; coming upon her mother at night, walking down a highway, facing traffic. These were all she would have had if there hadn't been that autumn evening with the bright lights and the red roses with thorns that pricked through her gloves. Traveling the circumference of the stadium with all those pale eyes following her and the glint of her crown. Then a big stripe of color on the home side, and Junior standing in the middle of it, his fist in the air, making sure that she saw him, that everybody saw him and understood that he was her father. And Elaine thrusting out at all of them a brave, large smile, the best that she could muster as the photographer flashed his bulb and Tyrone waved, eyes bright behind his thick glasses, and stole a kiss that was captured for the yearbook.

Elaine could never remember whether it was only in her dreams or in reality that she saw Luther on the sidelines. He was watching her, but he wasn't smiling, and when he turned and moved off she saw who'd been standing behind him all along. That white girl, the same one, with the long wavy hair and blue eyes. She watched Elaine too, even after Luther was gone, and when Elaine's car stopped in front of the home side, she cheered with everyone else. Cheered so that Elaine imagined she heard it specifically, apart from the other din, a high sharp cry.

It had taken her several weeks, after Cincinnati and Junior's tirade and moving a tenth of her wardrobe into Annie's cedar closet in the hall, for her to ask Luther the question she saw now should have been asked from the start.

"What happened to that white girl?"

Luther was eating a pork chop that she'd burned in Crisco because Annie was over looking at Netty's new couch.

"What do you mean, happened to her?" Luther replied, unable to keep the annoyance out of his voice. "Far as I know, she's still alive."

"To the two of you. It wasn't like you were trying to hide it."

Luther rose and put his plate in the sink. What had he thought? This was marriage; someone asking you questions always.

"That's over, OK?" he said finally. "It wasn't nothing. She's gone."

"Gone? Where?"

"I don't know. Columbus or someplace." He turned to her and got the first good look he'd ever had. He had either admired her from a distance or been pressed flush up to her in bed, so that he'd never had a normal range view of her, like this, sitting in flat sunlight. He saw that she had freckles on her nose and tiny ears and a slightly discolored tooth you would really see if she was smiling, which she wasn't. He softened when she twisted her ring and looked down.

"Look, we're married now. Nobody's asking you about Tyrone."

"There's nothing to ask about Tyrone, that's why."

To Luther's immense relief, Annie opened the front door just then and let a cold blast of air in through the two rooms to the kitchen.

"Hey, mama," he said as she came in and kissed them both, then walked automatically to the stove.

"Luther, why didn't you wait for me instead of burning up my pans?" she asked.

"I did it," Elaine said in a miserable tone.

ANNIE'S back began to ache when she got up in the morning; sometimes her legs gave way when she tried to stand. With all her baking, she'd gained weight in the last months, but she didn't know how much. Her bathroom scales were stuck at sixty and only went up to one hundred and ten. She couldn't bring herself to throw them out—or much of anything else—so that her house contained, more or less, the sum total of the possessions of her life.

No wonder she was having a hard time finding a place for Elaine's fancy clothes. When they'd tried to stuff more in the hall closet last week, a hat box with the veil from Annie's wedding, a patent leather purse, and Netty's christening dress had rained down upon them, in that order.

Elaine had given a sharp little laugh as she stooped down and picked everything up, dawdling over the crochet work on the dress. Annie'd stood watching her, wondering why she wasn't offering it for the baby, her grandchild. She told herself that she was ready to love Elaine at any time, but somehow it continued not to happen. They had an odd effect on each other; whenever they were in each other's company, they both grew tired. Elaine could blame this on her pregnancy, but Annie had nothing so solid. In many ways she empathized with Elaine, who was obviously feeling the same restlessness Annie'd experienced after first becoming a wife. The heat of her brief courtship had primed her for something more than pregnancy and a house of dusty rooms.

Now that Loretta was gone and Luther came home less than ever, Annie felt at a loss as to where to fasten her newly burgeoning hope. But it still blew around her, a small, prevailing gust, even when she and Elaine parted at the breakfast table and went their separate ways, back to bed. Annie had to wrap her arms around herself under the covers in order to quiet it down; it was imperative now, more than ever, that she sleep and dream.

TWO months after the wedding Luther received his first and only letter from Loretta. Annie had it in front of her, unopened, when he walked into the kitchen, looking at it as if she were trying to decipher the envelope.

"What are you gonna do?" she asked him.

"Read it," he said, taking it, and without thinking, walked to his bedroom and pulled the shower curtain tight. The letter said the baby was due in less than a month, that Loretta wasn't allowed to see it, and that afterwards she was being shipped directly to a private school out of state. At the end, she wrote: "I dream about us all, like some crazy puzzle that's cut wrong and can't ever be put back together. Sweet Luther, at least we managed this."

After he read the letter, he couldn't get off the bed. He buried his face in his pillow, wondering if there were some molecules, some dust particles of Loretta that still could be there from the past. He tried to think so, but it was difficult to imagine, considering how often Annie washed the sheets. And that was how Elaine found him, fast asleep, several hours later; Annie had already been up and taken the letter, which she folded neatly and placed in a sugar tin in the kitchen cabinet.

III

LUTHER kept track of deeds and wills and loans over the years, but he never knew what happened to that letter; he had been relieved it was gone when Elaine woke him that day, and assumed Annie had done something with it; it didn't matter—he already knew it, from that one reading, by heart. Throughout the years, it continued to annoy him that it was the only one he received, that he was evidently so easy to forget.

He was aware that he had changed remarkably since his marriage, that he'd become by all appearances, the perfect middle-class husband: prudent, marginally faithful, newly religious. The religion he felt, but couldn't explain; it was one of those things. The seed of it had been deposited long ago and had recently exploded under Elaine's tireless tutelage. He had accompanied her to church from the beginning, but always as a fatherly duty. And then one Sunday as he was sitting with a wandering mind, thinking of a haircut he'd given the day before and pondering the deacon's wife's thighs, something had happened. The voice of the minister had broken through to him, as if earplugs had been snatched from his head, and he discerned in the man's predictable and repetitive pronouncements something he was ready to hear. His right leg twitched and he shook it out in front of him, muttering to Elaine that it must have fallen asleep. But it wouldn't stop, and for this and other reasons, he got up minutes later with the rest of the devout and went up to the front of the church to be saved. He did not let Elaine follow—she was long saved anyway, and the thing he disliked most about marriage was her continual wifely presence always behind him; it gave him an ache.

Later that afternoon when they returned home, Elaine made him a deluxe roast-beef dinner, with extra gravy and mashed potatoes, unable to hide her pleasure. After they had eaten, she sank down in front of his chair and began crying weakly, a gesture that seemed almost Biblical and didn't fail to touch him.

"I always knew you had the spirit in you," she wept. "I've been praying for this for years."

Her saying that ruined it a bit for him; he didn't like to be predictable, and even after all this time, he couldn't help imagining Loretta's reaction had she seen him on his knees, reduced at an altar. But it had been a heavy, dulling meal that they had just eaten, and in his inertia, Luther allowed himself to take his wife to their tiny bedroom and make methodical love to her before falling off into a deep, troubled sleep.

He dreamed of Loretta that afternoon, as he often did, standing in front of Annie's house, telling him something he couldn't understand. He woke with a leaden need to find her and their child, a feeling that often dogged him for weeks. He had no idea where she was by now, barely knew where to begin. As the weeks went on, he tried praying—that he would quit searching the crowds at shopping malls, on game shows, at checkout lines, for the amalgam of his and Loretta's face. He prayed that he would appreciate the obedient wife and obedient children he already had, right there, aching to be appreciated. But his family was so easy; they looked up at him during one of his rages like the most obsequious of species. The praying didn't work, he quickly con-cluded, but he did not want to consider the implications of that.

ELAINE JOHNSON BIGGS—she signed her name Mrs. Biggs, but continued to think of herself in private in this expanded way—had somewhere along the line dedicated her life to watching her husband. She watched him from the moment he got out of bed each morning and presented his butt to her, each cheek as round as the iron skillets over her range, to when he walked in at night to their A-frame on Calumet where she'd made her small paths, from the bedroom, to the kitchen, to the window, all day. After all these years, she remained astounded that they'd married and that it had lasted this long and still couldn't shake the feeling, even after two sons and a mortgage and a diamond welded onto her wedding ring, that it didn't have much to do with her.

She and Luther were back in his childhood home while Annie was being hospitalized for angina when she discovered Loretta's letter in a sugar canister as she was fixing lunch for her sons. It was not only the intimacy of the note that shocked her—she and Luther had never written anything to each other—but the real-ization that the bond between the two of them had been blighted, and she knew that anything blighted, even the tamest thing, eventually deepens. Although it disturbed her, she vowed not to mention it to Luther, who wouldn't even notice her pensiveness; he was sunk into one of his cyclic depressions—this one due, in part, she thought, by his mother's hospitalization and the fact that their most recent child had not been a girl.

"It's supposed to be the other way around. Men are supposed to want sons," she said in a teasing voice when he had brought the baby to her for the first time, his face like a stone.

"I don't care how it's *supposed* to be, Elaine," he said, depositing the brown snail of a body on her chest. She had hated him then, hot and briefly, for being unable to rise out of himself even momentarily in order to dole out a little assurance, a bit of love. She watched in despair as the child squirmed on her chest like a mole, and did not even want to bestow it with a name, not alone. This is another one I'll have to worry over, she thought, another who I don't understand and am not supposed to. I would've liked a girl myself; I'm sick to death of boys and men.

Since then, she'd tried to convince herself that their lives were somehow getting better—Luther had opened a beauty salon that he owned and managed, allowing her to quit her full-time job; he was going to church and staying home in the evenings, occasionally even showing interest in their sons. But now simply unfolding an old piece of ruled paper had brought it all back.

DESPITE her resolve, Elaine broke down by dinner and admitted to finding the letter, telling Luther with a face so full of accusation that he'd had to turn away. He could not forgive her face—it said that she wanted his past, as well as his present, tied up in a bundle as neat as the garbage, resting carefully in their living room with its tweed chairs and weak lights. It said that she thought he had promised more than he ever would promise—for thoughts that never strayed, for a desire that stopped with her, like a slammed door at the end of a hallway.

"So you found it," he said, looking away. "What do you want me to say?"

Elaine only stared at him hopelessly, sitting in her madonna position, her head hung, their second child in her lap. It's all a front, he thought. What more can she possibly want? The truth was that everything about her had rankled him lately. Cleaning out a drawer last week, he had found old thank-you cards for wedding presents that for some reason she had never sent; her keeping them all those years annoyed him in itself; but it was more what she said:

"Thank you so much for the sheets and pillow cases. We really need them and the bright colors fit in so nice with the colors we planned for the bedroom."

Luther did not even remember those sheets and had never planned a bedroom, with anyone. And then he realized how long Elaine had been speaking for him, aligning an imaginary version of him in her life. I need to see Loretta, he thought as he read the notes. I need to see her before I forget who the hell I am.

IT was now late on a cold December night, several days before Christmas, and Luther was sitting on a swivel chair in his beauty parlor, waiting for Loretta to arrive.

"It won't do any good," she'd said when he'd finally reached her after a long, twisting search for her number in another state, another town. "Why don't you just leave me in your memory where I belong."

"And what about the baby? Where am I supposed to put that?"

"Just leave it, like I have. Plus, she's not a baby anymore."

"She? What do you mean, she? I didn't think you knew."

"I wasn't supposed to, but you do. Whether anyone tells you or not."

"I can just see you," Luther said suddenly, incited by the sound of her voice. "The way you used to be in bed." He went on, describing the feel of her lips, the fall of her hair, and Loretta, both embarrassed and gratified, did not make him stop, realizing that he was the only one who remembered her like this, who knew her in that way, then. Luther talked on, asking her questions, the answers to which he didn't want to hear. Except that she was unmarried now. He heard that; the fact that she was divorced he didn't dwell on. He was annoyed when she finally asked about his marriage, an intrusive fact that he had to acknowledge. After that, their conversation faltered, as if Elaine had actually walked into the space between them, bowing her head, a child at either side. But by then Luther had already convinced Loretta to come see him when she came home to have Christmas with her family; just for an hour, he swore, just this once. And even though it involved meeting in the cold darkness of his basement beauty salon, he somehow got her to agree.

LUTHER forgot all the things he intended to say to her from the moment he saw the tip of her leather boots descend the steps into his parlor.

"Loretta," was all he could think of as he walked up to take her in his arms, feeling for the first time how small she was; her head only came to his chest, near his heart. Later, when they had separated and were moving in and out of the dim basement light as he showed her around, Luther could not help noticing how she'd changed, particularly her face. Age, he thought in spite of himself. This is what they mean when they talk about how white folks age.

"And these are the hair dryers," he finished lamely when they had circled the room. He had managed to guide them in front of a mirrored wall, but Loretta wouldn't look up.

"Whoever thought you'd be a hairdresser," she said in a strange tone, sitting down on one of the chairs.

"Yeah, imagine," he said moving close to her. "I'd like to do yours."

"Oh, mine," she said grabbing a bunch of it as if it weren't her own. "We better leave mine as it is. Luther," she said then, looking at him directly. "You see what I mean, don't you? We don't have anything to say to each other now."

"But you're not even trying," he said, suddenly angered. "You haven't asked about Annie or how I'm feeling or . . . anything."

"But I already know what you'd say. You'd tell me Annie is fine, but she's getting older. You'd say you're fine. There's nothing to talk about."

She stood, moving away from him, for good, he saw. "And we're never going to find that child, Luther. You know that. All this is too hard. Let's not even try."

As she talked, Luther's mind wandered, as it did when any woman talked, and he found himself imagining Elaine, standing in their mortgaged house several blocks away; at this hour of the night she would be cleaning her face with Noxema, gradually washing away the white until her skin was brown again. He imagined Annie in bed with her dreambook, Nettie pulling on her strawberry hair. He saw Loretta, then and now, and tried to imagine their tall, bronze, faceless child. So many women, he thought, leaning toward him, then pulling away. You never really had one, not all for your own, not ever for long.

AFTER leaving the beauty salon, Loretta sat in her car at the corner of Sugar Street and thought about history. By leaving school when she had, she'd missed a class on the Roman Empire. It had been scheduled for History II at the beginning of the second semester, but she'd been on her own timetable by then, and her mother'd suggested that this break was the best time for her to leave. There had been so many things to regret by then that Loretta had latched onto this one, for convenience—that she had missed what might have been her only chance to learn about this time. As a girl she'd gone to a grade school named Marcus Aurelius, and she'd always meant to discover exactly who he was.

Each night as she'd lain on her cot at the home for unwed mothers, her mind had skipped over all she did not know: Was it a beech or elm or chestnut that stood outside her window; a finch or sparrow's song? Surely there were constellations over that part of Ohio, but how did you see their pattern when it all seemed like random light? Even then Loretta saw she'd never know any of this, possibly in all her life. This was what she'd regret—more than her mother's face at the doctor's door, or Annie's back as she'd said goodbye, even more than the child still lodged there, south of her heart.

About the Author

Lynn Lauber grew up in northwestern Ohio and graduated from Ohio State University. Her stories have appeared in such literary magazines as *Stories* and *Fiction Network* as well as in several anthologies, and one of her stories was broadcast on the BBC World Service Short Story series. She currently works as a book abridger, editor, and teacher. She lives in Piermont, New York.